SYLVIE GINESTET

THE QUEST

© Sylvie Ginestet 2014
All rights reserved.

ISBN : 978-2-930756-03-5
First published in French under the title "Le Miracle' by Editions Azimuts in 2012.
Translated from French by "Intuitive Translations", Torquay, United Kingdom.

SYLVIE GINESTET

THE QUEST

A special thanks to Graham

1

My foot was in terrible pain and I had no idea where I was.

I sat up in my bed and groped around for the bedside table, hoping to find a lamp which would allow me to get my bearings. Fortunately, I found one, which worked. Certainly, the light from its bulb wasn't very bright, nevertheless it was enough for me to realise that I wasn't at home.

The pain was a stabbing one, it was now working its way along to my ankle. A small fine scab had formed on the top of my foot. What had happened to me, and why was I here? I tried to remember, but the last twenty-four hours were vague. It was like being in a fog, I really couldn't remember anything!

Little by little, my vision became used to the low light; I began to have a look around the room. The furniture was antique, I could distinguish a wardrobe and a writing desk of a certain era. Which one? A mystery... The bed in which I found myself was big, much larger than my own. It was a four-poster bed decorated with Bordeaux drapes.

The more I looked around me, the more anxious I became... Then I tried to get up, but I hadn't the strength for it.

I wasn't wearing my usual clothes, just a long white nightgown. This only increased my anxiety. I had without doubt been the victim of an accident, but in this case why wasn't I at the hospital? I've always had a rather confident nature, to the point of readily following someone in the street, but this, it was a little too much, and now it was worrying me.

I tried to rationalise calmly. Above all, I mustn't panic. I was still trying to grasp the situation when someone knocked at the door. The person entered without even waiting for an answer. Automatically, I pulled the covers up to my chin.

"Good evening, Miss."

I answered with a distrusting stammer. The man was tall and had nothing about him of an orderly or a nurse's aide, he was dressed as a butler. His look was black, and frightening.

"I bring you your soup," he announced most straightforwardly.

"Could you...?"

"Sir should be home soon, I will inform him that you wish to see him."

I frowned; a heap of questions were cropping up.

"Thank you, but...Where am I? How long have I been here and why?"

"You came last night with Sir. Here, you have a bell should you need anything."

He pointed to a small old-fashioned red velvet tassel which seemed straight out of another time. He spoke strangely. I was becoming more and more worried.

"Could I have a telephone? My family has to be worried, I absolutely have to call them. And anyway, who is "Sir"? What happened to me?"

I was nearing hysteria. Him, he remained impassive, and answered none of my questions.

"Call me if you need anything," he concluded dispassionately.

"But answer me, good God!"

It was a waste of time... He put the tray on a small table next to the door and left the room, locking up behind him.

One thing was for sure: I had to get to my feet and leave this place, whatever it took. For what reason was I being held prisoner?

I tried again to get up but I felt very weak. I managed finally to sit on the edge of the bed. My feet couldn't even touch the floor and there was no sign of my clothes! Nevertheless, I had to find them if I wanted to leave this place.

Putting my foot down turned out to be a real torture. I walked slowly towards the window using the furniture to help relieve my pain. A little fresh air would do me a world of good, it would help me to see things more clearly.

The curtains, matching the bed, were very beautiful, very heavy, made from velvet like we don't find any more nowadays. I positioned myself between the drapes, hands at face level, and little by little I discovered a wonderful landscape which I hadn't expected. The sun had set, but lights illuminated the garden tastefully. In every sense, this confirmed that I'd found myself in a chateau. The furniture, the gardens... There was no possible doubt.

I wanted to open the French window: It was locked. So I left the curtains partly open. The light which penetrated into the room brought a little serenity to this enclosed space, and to myself, who sorely needed it.

I felt a more painful stab in my foot. I was tired, nearing the point of crying. I then ventured to the wardrobe. Miracle! My jeans and my pullover were there. I managed to slip into them. Dressed in my own clothes, I felt a little less vulnerable. This nightgown was pretty, but I felt ill-at-ease with the idea that someone may have undressed me.

Before anything else, I had to revive myself. The soup would at least give me some strength, I hoped. I gulped it down but then I realised suddenly that it might have been drugged. Anyway, it was too late now, and besides I'd already started feeling my energy coming back to me...

I put an ear to the door in order to listen for the slightest sound, but without any success. Then I just leant there and scrutinised the room, with a view to unearthing a way out. The sound of tyres on the gravel path interrupted my investigations. I returned to the window.

A man stepped out from a car. I knew this silhouette. But... It was Darren! I immediately knocked on the window, in the hope that he would hear me and come to save me. The man in black came to speak to him. He raised his head towards me, and I felt some hope. I kept watching them: They entered inside the chateau.

The key turned in the lock, the door opened slowly. This time, there was no knock. I stayed near the curtains.

"Good evening," a soft and familiar voice said to me.

I tried to glimpse the figure in the light beyond the door. A tall black shape was staring at me and waiting for my invitation to enter.

"Good evening Darren. Why am I locked in? Where are we?"

"You're at my home, Lilly, and if you're locked in, it's for your own safety."

"My safety?"

"Don't worry... May I enter or am I condemned to remain standing between two rooms?"

This remark made me smile, which encouraged him to come into the bedroom. He took a chair and sat down near the bed without saying a word. He was content with just looking at me.

"This is your home!" I said curtly. "Would you care to explain everything to me please?"

"Why are you up and dressed?"

"I don't remember what happened to me last night. Before seeing you down below, I believed myself to be the prisoner of a madman, or I don't know what else. I was already formulating a plan for saving myself."

He seemed amused by what I said. For my part, I didn't find it funny, but I now felt reassured. It struck me that he was beautiful, the subdued light let me glimpse his fine, regular and symmetrical features. I didn't remember everything, but this face and the sweetness which he gave off reminded me about the spirit of the choice which I had made.

He smiled tenderly to me.

"We left the club to come here as planned, however everything didn't go how I... How we expected."

"What's the problem?"

At this precise moment, I felt a new stab in my foot and my question finished with a grimace which could hardly have escaped him. In one bound, he was in front of me.

"Let me see this foot."

"How do you know it's my foot which hurts?"

"Because it was me who injured you," he replied, embarrassed.

I sat down on the bed and allowed him to examine my wounds. How and why had he hurt me? Ah the memories began to return to me... The club, the car, then the blackout.

"It's serious?"

"A little infected, but nothing nasty. It must be down to your medical history. Don't worry, we're going to take care of it as quickly as possible."

Directly, he pulled the red tassel. A few moments later someone knocked at the door.

"Come in, Hector!"

Standing in front of the door, Hector waited for his orders. This man frightened me, he was glacial; no smile, no emotion came from him.

"Go and look for something to disinfect Lilly's foot. You'll find what's necessary in my case which is in the chest of drawers in my office. The blue case!" He ordered, without even turning his head.

"Yes, Sir."

Hector had already left.

Something had happened and I had absolutely no memory of it, but Darren knew... He knew everything. Now I too needed to know. I repeated my question.

"Can you tell me more now? What didn't work out? Has it something to do with my request? Why can't I remember anything?"

He sat on the edge of the bed and stared at me, yet I didn't lower my eyes.

"Yes, it's to do with your request but I can't tell you more. In fact, I don't even know the answer myself. How far back can you remember?"

"I know neither how I came to be here, nor since when. Also, I don't remember how I got injured, even if I now understand what it relates to. However, I can't remember you doing it."

"It's all right, it'll heal quickly. Don't worry. I'm more worried about the second stage, the one which didn't come about. Whatever happens, just know that the reason I accepted your deal was for your survival. That's the one and only reason, Lilly."

His last reflection hardly did anything to reassure me.

Hector was patiently waiting for us to stop talking. Darren felt his presence and turned his head toward him while getting up. Hector put the case at his feet on the floor and left as discreetly as he'd come.

"I didn't know you were a doctor!"

"Ha-ha! Do I seem like a doctor?"

"Well, a bit, yes. Especially so with this case."

He looked at me with an air of amusement.

"You won't find any doctor able to heal these wounds. I'll apply some antiseptic so try not to touch it. Also, take these two pills with a little water, please."

He handed me two white capsules without any distinguishing marks, as well as a glass of water.

I swallowed them without hesitation. They were tasteless. In this moment, I was certain that he didn't want to poison me.

"You should heal quickly," he said with a reassuring voice, while packing away his potions.

He closed his case, raised his head and said:

"Now, it's time for you to get some rest. Tomorrow, you'll be able to walk. We'll go for a walk in the park."

"You know, honestly… I really wish it had worked."

"Me too. Goodnight, Lilly."

He gently kissed me on the forehead and left the bedroom.

I was alone again in this room. Certainly, I now knew why I was here. The only thing which tormented me was that we may have done it all for nothing... And still, there was this wound!

Since my early childhood, I'd always had a fragile health. I would catch all the diseases which other children would never get, and of course it was always more complicated to treat. I presented a very unusual case for the doctors, however I survived all of this since I was quite used to it. Above all, I would always come out of it stronger and more resistant to the illness.

But by continually enduring and suffering in silence — as one never speaks, or rarely so, about this kind of health condition — you end up finding yourself unable ever to know whether something much worse or unusual is going on. That's why, for six months I fought against an invisible disease which was slowly making its way around my body. The doctors couldn't find anything, and the results of any examinations would come back negative. In brief: I had nothing to go on.

Our family doctor concluded that I was suffering from depression. Everything was coming from me and it was all in my head. After all, maybe my mind had finally given up and forsaken me? I didn't believe this, as it was simply inconceivable for me that my mind could now wreak so much havoc after everything my body had already endured.

I was able to listen to my body but the opposite wasn't true: My body seemed to have a plan of its own. It didn't matter that I kept repeating to myself: "It's nothing, it's in my head, I'm fine and well", something was definitely wrong.

On the advice of my doctor - after all, we have to believe them - I went for the first and only time to meet with a psychologist. I'm not really the kind of person who likes to expose her private life to a complete stranger, even less when you can never get a proper response. Once again I had to come to my senses: Psychologists weren't made for me.

I was back at the beginning. I had refused all the drugs which supposedly would have made me feel better. This was one of the best decisions I ever made to this day.

I needed to know what I was doing, what I was thinking, and especially what I was feeling. I kept notes on the disease's progression, writing down the slightest detail in a notebook, however my doctor stuck to his earlier diagnosis: I was suffering from depression, period. Case closed.

The first clear and visible symptom appeared two years ago, during the summer. I was working in my office when suddenly the room started spinning. Everything was whirling around in such a frenzied waltz that my only relief was to sit down in a corner, crouched against the wall making sure I wouldn't hurt myself by falling. Yet, even with my eyes closed, it kept on swirling. A very painful sensation, believe me!

The diagnosis of the paramedics came: Rotatory Vertigo. They advised me to get a complete check-up since those disorders are caused by an abnormality affecting the balance organs such as the brain, the nerves or the ears. Yet again, my doctor sent me back for a brain MRI scan which of course didn't show any lesion. Then he prescribed rest — the smartest thing he ever did during this whole period!

A few days later, my head exploded. It was too late to do anything to prevent it. The diagnosis was irrevocable, harsh and painfully true: "Stroke". I found myself bedridden but alive. Well, almost…

A long re-education had to begin. I had to learn everything again from scratch. The left side of my body was lifeless and my expressions limited. The irony was that only my brain was working properly. To put it plainly, I could feel one hundred percent of all this. A spirit living in a half dead body. There, I admit it, it was really just all too much!

The following nine months were a tough and relentless battle from which I came out almost victorious: I was able to walk and I could speak without dribbling. Seen from the outside, I was back to my normal self. However, while everybody else thought all was well, deep down I knew that things would never be the same again.

This hell lasted for two years, until I told myself that it couldn't continue any more. I was ceaselessly tired, and in truth very few people understood it. They more readily took me to be an idler than a person who had probably suffered irreversible damage. As long as we're not completely paralysed, blind or on life support, people either don't understand or just don't want to understand.

I was tired of having to justify myself all the time, of having to beg for some hope of a normal life.

I had to find a solution.

2

My quest for the inconceivable began last summer. After all, it couldn't just "be" a legend, because as it's well known; all legends are based on real facts.

I avoided going on the internet, for fear of finding all the idiocies of the world on the subject. Thus, I decided to take a sabbatical, which was granted to me without batting an eyelid. So I now had six months to find what I was looking for.

I began surveying the streets. I observed the slightest sensitive detail which might suggest a lead. Of course, I'd chosen Paris, the pinnacle that it is, of the world of the night. Considering what I knew, I said to myself that night-time would be the most appropriate moment for my initiative. So I'd noted down on a sheet of paper a list of establishments which seemed to meet my criteria. My choice was just based on the name. I wasn't expecting miracles, but this was a start at least.

I spent my time in clubs, some more or less murky or shabby than others. These risky outings had the virtue of putting me in a good mood, since sometimes that was pushed to extremes. Alas! Nothing there was authentic.

I exhausted my first list at the end of August; I started immediately with the second, that of the bars and clubs.

In the middle of September, a glimmer of hope appeared when I met a certain "Vic", who I got on well with. He was different to other people, a little bit silly in fact, but let's say more credible in his role. He was the barman in a particular club called "Blood Blues Jazz Club". I must admit that this place was lost at the bottom of my list, my not being a fan of Jazz sufficiently to spend the night there. Also, the name was perhaps not suggestive enough. Which just goes to show that first ideas are sometimes wrong. But with hindsight, this name was excellent!

I settled down at the bar, on a high stool with a backrest, which seemed very comfortable, then I ordered a "Corona".

I wouldn't know how to explain why his look drew my attention. There was something particular about him; the colour of his eyes perhaps, or the whiteness of his skin, the thinness of his fingers. It formed a whole. He brought me my beer (without a glass, oops!) and I turned to have a look around the place. A Jazz group were playing a well-known Armstrong piece. Now that my eyes had become used to the half-light, I could distinguish some customers scattered here and there.

The stage was at the back of the room, but the acoustics were excellent. It was a change from the techno-clubs, with their sound system full-blast and DJ in a trance, or the old-fashioned bars full of winos.

An aisle led straight ahead to the stage. On each side, tables were surrounded by leather armchairs. The place was cozy. For good measure, everything was shrouded in a smoke almost obligatory for a Jazz club.

When they began the second piece, I said to myself that I would certainly stay longer than planned. Was it the beer, the music, the atmosphere? I don't know, but I felt good. I decided therefore to settle myself in. I asked for the menu so I could eat a little, and put my bag down on the counter near me. At that moment, I noticed an ashtray. I didn't need to ask the question: The waiter looked at me with a nod of his head. What was more, I could smoke! He would face steep fines, because the law no longer permitted smoking in public places, but after all, perhaps Jazz clubs benefited from a special dispensation, for the sake of atmosphere!

I took the notepad out of my bag, to put down on paper my first impressions of this place. Such praise! And above all this feeling of not being far from my aim. Whatever happened, I would return.

I started my sandwich and my second Corona, when the group had a break. Suddenly a strange silence descended. The barman (Vic) put on a Sting CD. "I don't drink coffee, I take tea my dear, I like my toast done on the side, and you can hear it in my accent when I talk, I'm an Englishman in New York". I adored this song, it suited the place well.

The musicians came over to settle down at the bar, their drinks were already waiting for them: Vic was a good barman. I don't know if they spent more time in cellars than on beaches, but they had all a porcelain complexion.

There were four of them. At the end of the bar, in front of me, sat the pianist. Tall, with short brown hair, he was wearing a checked shirt, with jeans and a waistcoat in blue. The double-bassist sat near the beer pumps. Of normal height, he had a goatee beard and long hair. The drummer remained standing in order to smoke a cigarette. He was dressed all in black, which highlighted his blond hair. He had fine features, I would say that he probably came from Northern Europe. Finally, the saxophonist sat just next to me, quietly sipping a beer. For me, he was the most beautiful of the four. He was refined, with manicured nails and long hair tied with a ribbon of black velvet. I was filled with admiration for such beauty. Furthermore, he seemed gentle and pleasant.

I was still looking at him, when he raised his head abruptly. I couldn't pretend to look somewhere else, it was too late.

"The music pleased you?" He asked.

"Yes, it was very good," I said blushing.

"It's the first time I've seen you here."

His look was piercing, intimidating. I tried not to lose my nerve.

"You're right. Do you appear here every evening?"

"No, only Wednesdays and Sundays," he answered, finishing his beer.

"Very good."

"You'll come again?"

His question surprised me.

"Certainly. Even if I'm not a Jazz fan, I found it very relaxing. Has this place been here for a long time?"

A wide smile lit up his face.

"Centuries."

"Oh! In that case, I'm late."

"Can I offer you another beer?" He asked, already raising his finger to call to Vic.

"No thank you. On the other hand, I'd love a coffee."

"Vic, two coffees, please."

"Here we go!" shouted the waiter at the end of the counter.

Suddenly, the bar seemed to me very busy, more alive. Vic brought us our coffees, humming another song by Sting.

"Me, I'm Darren," said the saxophonist, offering me his hand.

"Lilly."

"Enchanted, Lilly."

"Likewise."

The touch of his hand gave me a shock. It was very cold, but I pretended not to notice anything and I returned his smile.

"What's your name shortened from?" He asked.

"It's not shortened, I was baptised with it. My mother adored this Christian name, and I love it too."

"Yes, it's very beautiful. Moreover, it suits you very well."

"Thank you. What's the origin of yours?"

"Irish"

"You have no accent at all."

"I've been in France for a long time."

"You don't miss your country?"

"No, I no longer have an attachment there. I sometimes return, but at the moment, I feel at home here."

"I didn't want to be indiscreet; we don't know each other, and here I am asking you lots of questions... It's most impolite of me. No doubt, it's the effect of the beer."

"I have to go back to play," he apologised.

He got up and added:

"But you owe me one question..."

"All right."

"Why are you here?"

His look was suddenly different. Was it the effect of the light or simply an impression?

"I'm looking for something unimaginable."

I couldn't believe it. Why had I answered this?

"I have to join them," He said, pointing to the band. "Goodbye, Lilly."

"Goodbye, Darren. Thank you for the coffee."

He was already on the stage.

I felt ridiculous. I suddenly realised that I hadn't considered the manner in which I would explain what I wanted to do, in case I found the person or the solution I was searching for. This seemed completely foolish to me, especially since I sensed I'd found something, or rather somebody.

I continued my searches over the following nights, but my thoughts always returned to the Jazz club and to this man. This affected my judgment, as I found my visits useless. I had the feeling that I was wasting my time. So on Saturday evening, I decided not to go out and I stayed in to listen to some music in peace.

The next day, I took the irrational decision to return to the Jazz club. I had nothing to lose: Either this man would ignore me, or he would speak to me. I'd know then if he could help me. My instinct; this was telling me to charge ahead. It encouraged me to confide in him: If he himself didn't have the solution, maybe he'd know somebody? But quite honestly, something told me that he had the means to help me. Assuming of course that he'd accept.

I'd imagined a plan of attack: I had to make him talk, to lead him into revealing himself, and so to ask me the questions. But I'd have to exercise caution, having seen his reaction during our first encounter.

I went back to the bar. Apparently, the concert hadn't started yet. The stage was empty, background music obscured the conversations, it was much busier than on Wednesday.

"My" seat in the bar was occupied by a man. Nevertheless, a quick glance around allowed me to spot a place among the armchairs, not far from the stage.

The table was free, I settled myself in. Two minutes later, Vic took my order. On his advice, I opted for the house cocktail, the "Bloody White", consisting essentially of Malibu and vanilla. He brought it to me, accompanied by peanuts and crisps. He seemed snowed under and I had neither the time nor the courage to ask him if the group were playing this evening.

I was keenly sipping my nectar. This cocktail was really gentle on the palate. It warmed my blood, without getting me drunk.

"Good evening Lilly."

I slowly turned my head to make him out against the light. My heart pounded. This time, I couldn't hold back, I had to speak to him. I didn't want him to think that I was here for another reason, let's say… More logical.

"Good evening Darren."

"On Sundays, we come on at 9pm. Hadn't I told you? I'm sorry. Have you been waiting for a while?"

"No, I found myself a good seat. Besides, it's nice here and the cocktail is delicious. There's no problem."

It's true; I felt relaxed, in spite of everything.

"Perfect! Hey, you're drinking a "Bloody White"? So; try the "Red", next time."

Then, he disappeared. How could he be certain that there would be a next time? It was becoming urgent that we talk, I didn't want him to be mistaken about my intentions.

A few minutes later, he reappeared on stage with the rest of the group. They were tuning their instruments, turning the pages of their scores. The audience became silent. After all, the people were there to listen to them.

"On the advice of Darren! He asked me to warn you: drink it slowly."

I jumped at Vic's words. I was so absorbed with watching the stage, that I hadn't heard him arrive.

"Oh! Thank you. That's it, a "Red"? It is really stronger?"

How did Vic know to bring the drink? They hadn't had time to speak to one another...

"Just different. Made with old Irish whiskey and cranberry."

"You have the number for a taxi, I hope?"

"You'll not be needing it," he concluded with a wink.

He left laughing. I scrutinised my glass, asking myself how my evening would end. One thing was certain: I had to stay lucid, otherwise he would understand nothing and I'd find myself at the madhouse in no time at all! I only hoped he'd give me more time than before.

They played continuously for an hour and a half. This audience was very different, more accompanying, more involved, they participated more. A woman came to sit down at my table. As the club was really full, I had no other choice but to accept. She was completely taken by the music; blonde, very beautiful, very proud.

They finished the concert to a thunder of applause. The woman near me, was standing. She smiled at me.

"It was brilliant, as ever. They're so good!"

"You're right."

I had no desire to get acquainted, I had a very specific purpose here. Small talk could wait until much later. The group dispersed around the room. Darren came towards us.

"Ah! I adore them! Darren you were all fantastic, this evening. Some new pieces, right?"

"Good evening, Marie. Yes, a few... Marie, I'd like to introduce you to Lilly. Lilly, this is my sister Marie. One of my most fervent admirers, as you might have noticed. I hope she didn't bother you?"

"Good evening Marie! No, not in the least."

I would never have guessed that they were brother and sister: She was as blonde as he was brown! Their only thing in common, now that I took an interest, was their gaze. An especially piercing look. Having said that, she posed me a problem: No question of discussing things with him if she stayed. Vic came and saved me without knowing it.

"Marie! It's been a while since I saw you, you must have millions of things to tell me? Join me in the bar."

"Vic? Yes, of course. Would you excuse me?"

She addressed this more to her brother. Vic took her by the waist, Darren kissed her on the forehead and they slipped away.

Darren turned towards me, he had an air of both exhaustion and relief. With his hand, he invited me to sit down again, from now on we would be face to face.

"She's sometimes a little bit absorbing, please excuse her"

"It's all right, she was silent until your arrival."

"Oh! In that case, you've avoided something dreadful," he added, smiling.

I had no idea of the way I was going to begin the conversation, so much of it seemed delicate. Lots of people came to congratulate him; they were discreet, but every interruption made me hesitant.

"What is your quest Miss Lilly?"

His question disconcerted me, I hadn't expected it at all. Logically, it should have been me starting off the conversation, it's me who should lead the dance!

"It's complicated to say, but it's very important to me. Swear that you won't mock me, and above all not to tell anybody."

"Why do you have confidence in me, Lilly? We don't know each other?"

"It's very true. But I'm following my intuition. Am I mistaken?"

"That all depends on what you're going to ask me. But since you've endured two hours of Jazz, it must be important."

This remark made me smile and relaxed me a little.

"I don't know where to start."

"At the beginning, wouldn't it be simplest? Try to relax and talk to me in your own words; express it as if you were saying it to yourself. If I don't understand, I'll interrupt you."

"Okay."

I got my breath back and tried hard to calm down. I was about to tell my life story to a man I'd known for only a few days. I was about to ask him for help with a subject which, maybe, didn't exist! I was ready to run away, but I didn't, because that wouldn't have let me move forward.

For an hour, I explained to him my health problems, my current state, and how hard it was for me. I furnished him with all the details of my pitiful life without falling into melodrama. He showed himself to be very patient, listening to me without a word, but with all his attention. At no time did he lose eye contact; and he never showed any sign of boredom.

Vic came to bring us fresh drinks, this came just at the right time. I was about to approach the sensitive subject. I held my glass in both hands, to warm me up. I was frozen by fear: Fear of his reaction, fear of the end of this conversation... Or rather this monologue. He must have realised it.

"Lilly, what you endured was painful and still is, if I understood properly. But for the moment, I don't see how I could help you. I'm not a doctor: I'm a musician! Granted, music sometimes brings about miracles, but in your case, it seems to me unlikely."

I looked him straight in the eyes, I tried to feel reassured. His look was soft, he didn't show pity for me. He even seemed sincere. If my intuition was right, if I managed to convince him, it would be wonderful; on the other hand, if I'd made a mistake, at least I would've got to know someone nice... But above all, I would feel ridiculous. I continued:

"I know. Anyway, a few months ago, I had an idea. At that time, it seemed excellent, but now that I have to express it, I'm not so sure about it; it now seems a bit far-fetched."

"What is this idea, Lilly?"

"I have no other choice: There's nothing medical left which can help me and my life's an ordeal. How many times hadn't I thought to..."

"Your idea, Lilly?"

I raised my head towards him, I thought he'd become impatient. But no... He wanted to help me to express myself. I looked down towards the ground and murmured:

"I need a miracle cure."

"Which one?"

He tilted his head to watch my eyes. His attitude made me smile.

"I don't know if it'll work."

"If you don't explain, I'll never know! Go on, you've said too much now."

"Oh! My God, it's so difficult... So crazy!"

He passed me a lit cigarette, I accepted it with great pleasure. After drawing some breaths, I felt ready. I closed my eyes and just said it all in one go.

"I'm not in search of immortality, I'm looking for serenity. I'm looking for a vampire that, with its bite, will cure me, will clean up my blood and will make me someone "normal"."

He put his glass down noisily on the table and got up. His look was icy, black. For the first time, I looked down out of fear. I told myself that I'd been right to come here. I was at the right place, but the game was far from being won.

I realised suddenly that the bar was closed and that we were alone. All the customers had left and, preoccupied by speaking, I hadn't noticed. Getting up, I spoke out:

"I'll let you think about my proposal."

I didn't dare to face him.

"What proposal? Who says that I'm a vampire?"

"You didn't contradict me, as far as I know? Here's my number."

I put a card with my address and phone number next to his glass, and headed for the exit.

I expected laughter, mockery, but not anger. As I arrived at the door, there he was. He'd got there in a lightning flash. I turned around to gauge the distance. How long had it taken me?

"Is it so absurd to want to live like everybody else?"

"It's not to live like everybody, Lilly. My world is not yours. Everything's different, even if over the centuries, we've adapted. We hide ourselves in the crowd, but there is still a danger, and not just a minor one."

He was wholly confirming what he truly was.

"Which one?"

"Humans."

"I represent no danger for you."

"Yes you do! The simple matter of believing in vampires, it's already a danger for us. If you found me, any ill-intentioned person can do it. I know now the reasons for your presence here, I knew when I first saw you that you were looking for something else. My instinct told me not to talk to you, but I believed that you wouldn't return."

"I can leave and never return, if you want. I won't say anything to anyone. Besides, who would believe me? However if you exist, others also exist, or am I mistaken?"

"There are a certain number of us, indeed. On the other hand, we're not all nice. Take care of yourself, Lilly."

Then, he opened the door, which gently closed the conversation.

I didn't turn around. I walked back to the small apartment which I was renting in Paris during my investigation. The positive point of this evening, was that they existed... HE existed. I'd made one step forward in my search, but one step back regarding the result. Would he call me back? I left him be for a few days. If he wouldn't do it, I'd start hunting again, but it would be a shame.

I was so lost in my thoughts, that I found myself in front of my door without really feeling that I'd covered the distance. My first reflex, every time I came in, was to look at the answering machine. There, I had three new messages. I didn't dare to listen to them... The fear of refusal, or simply the fear that he hadn't called, although a phone call so soon wasn't very likely.

The first message turned out to be from my mother: "How are you? What are you doing?" The usual questions, always the same throughout the years. The second came from a double glazing salesman. The last one said this:

"Lilly, you confided in me without holding back. I could have, I should have had a different reaction. Understand me... Your request was so unusual, so strange, so inconceivable... You were right, it's crazy. I didn't think anyone would ever ask me such a thing. I never thought of being considered anything other than a predator. I must admit that it frightens me. I never put myself in the role of a saviour. Your idea isn't bad, but I don't think I'm the one you're looking for."

The message finished with those words. I listened to it dozens of times before I went to sleep. I couldn't help myself from crying: I had found something, but I didn't hold much hope for it being the solution. He'd refused, this was clear. What should I do? Continue searching? Give up after this first failure? But was it really the first one? Every place I'd visited - normal clubs, in fact - they represented so many failures. But here, this was different: He was exactly the man I'd been searching for! Could I find another person like him in the little time that I had left? Why had I told him everything?

The night might bring me insight, so I decided to sleep: The following day, I would consider what to do next.

Upon waking, I made the decision to abandon this avenue. The time had come for a more conventional approach. I would maybe find other leads in books or on the internet. Now I had more information; I knew above all that they really did exist.

I walked around Paris, it was a nice day. How sweet life could be sometimes! The second hand booksellers were still open, the tourists hadn't left the city yet. The quays were my favourite place, they were steeped in history.

"Are you looking for something, my dear lady?" One of the booksellers asked me.

I looked at his stall over his shoulder. He had nothing but postcards there.

"I doubt that you can help me."

"Just ask me," he insisted.

"I'm researching about vampires in Paris."

"I don't have anything, but go and see Albert: The third kiosk on your right. Where there's a big gargoyle, you see?"

"Yes. Thank you very much, sir."

"A pleasure!"

He bid me goodbye, with a gesture of raising his cap. So I went over to see Albert. His kiosk was themed on the mysteries of Paris. Many works on Notre-Dame, and the catacombs. On the other hand, I saw nothing on vampires. His books were beautiful, but expensive.

"May I help you?"

"Your friend, over there, told me you might have something to offer me about vampires."

"Hmm, let me have a look..."

He began rummaging around in his boxes. It certainly wasn't the kind of enquiry that he'd get every day. He emerged with an old book which was titled "Vampires of the eighteenth century" and handed it to me. I began to flick through the pages, when I sensed a presence very near, much too near to me. I turned around with a jump to face Darren. What was he doing here?

"All this, its utter nonsense," he said to me.

"Oh yes, why's that?"

"It's pure fiction. Vampires don't exist, Lilly!"

I put the book back down, apologised to the seller and turned back towards Darren... But he'd disappeared. I looked to the seller for confirmation:

"You saw him as well, right?"

"Yes, of course. Are you okay, miss?"

"Yes thanks. Have a good day!"

I looked around again, but couldn't see him anywhere. What was he looking for?

I went back up an alley towards the Boulevard Saint Germain, I needed to eat something. I knew a pub in the area. In any case, if he'd wanted to frighten me, he'd succeeded, because I realised I was trembling. I turned around once again, but he'd disappeared for good.

Thank God, the pub was open! Luckily, I also found a pavement table and ordered my meal.

I had a cigarette in the meantime, and had an impression of seeing Darren in front of me. Was his being there just a coincidence? Or was he following me? But in this case, whatever for? Surely he'd refused to help me? So, the matter was closed. Nevertheless, I began to feel afraid; maybe I represented a danger for him. That said, he knew more about me than I did about him. Me, I knew two things: His first name and his secret.

The waiter brought my sandwich and my mint soda. I couldn't manage to swallow any.

"You have to eat, Lilly."

I jumped up, such that I almost fell off my seat. He was here! How had he done it? Obviously, he was following me.

"In God's name, Darren, what are you playing at? Do you want to frighten me to death?"

"It would be a solution to your problem," he said with a wink.

"That's not funny! You didn't believe me, anyway. Why are you following me?"

"To be honest, I came across you by accident in the quays," he continued, looking at his nails.

"Can I believe you?"

"Of course. Why, I would follow you?"

"I don't know."

I leant over to whisper to him:

"Maybe I'm now an embarrassing witness; perhaps I know too much?"

"Witness of what?"

"You know very well what."

I left a ten euro note on the table and got up. This time, it was me ending the conversation. He was sowing doubts in me, but above all he was really frightening me now. I didn't understand his attitude. I went back to my apartment without seeing him again.

The next day, I returned to buy the book from the second hand bookseller. This book was an incredible source of information. Now, I understood why Darren had dissuaded me from buying it. I spent the next few days reading it, it was really fascinating.

On Saturday at about 11pm, I decided to have a break and I went for a walk in the "Marais". According to the book, this district was steeped in history concerning vampires.

Even in the evening, the district was very alive. I passed in front of the Hotel de Sens, a very beautiful edifice restored long ago by the Paris City Hall. It still had its dungeon and was splendidly lit at night.

I went back up the Rue du Figuier in the direction of the Place de Vosges. The Rue Saint Antoine was swarming with people, despite the lateness of the hour. When I came to the square, I sat on a bench and soaked up the atmosphere of the place. With my eyes closed, I just breathed in the night air, I felt great. Ah! If only my life was always this way!

"You shouldn't walk alone at night."

I opened my eyes in panic, but I couldn't see anybody there. Then, I got up and went back home in a hurry. My peace of mind had now given way to an inner terror. My heartbeat was out of control.

He appeared suddenly in front of me. I stopped dead. The feeble glow from a streetlight revealed his face. He stifled my cries with his hand and pushed me into a large doorway. He no longer looked like the Darren I knew. His face wasn't gentle any more, he looked more like an animal. Yes, he was well and truly a predator. The proof of it was right in front of my eyes. He had chased after me, I was terrified. He had so many advantages over me: Suppleness, speed and particularly strength.

I didn't dare look him in the eyes, but he forced me to. I felt tears streaming down my cheeks. I had gone too far with him and, in a second, he could kill me. I realised my error, alas a little too late.

"Yes, I am a predator, I'm no kind of saviour. Get out this idea of your head before it's too late. Drop it now!" He whispered with a voice from beyond the grave.

I couldn't articulate one word, I was paralysed with fear. He released me and just left me there. I sat on the ground, huddled myself up, and I cried. I stayed there for several hours. I found it impossible to move or even to think, the fear was too intense.

At dawn, I felt somebody putting their hands on my knees. I slowly raised my head. A sweet and familiar face was looking at me.

"Come on, Lilly, I'll take you back home."

Vic was standing in front of me and smiled at me. How had he known I was here?

"I'm not sure I can get up, I'm sorry."

"Try" he said, offering me his hand.

I leant on him all the way to his car. Barely sitting, I started crying again silently, my head turned outwards. Darren had won: I gave up. I hadn't succeeded, it was obvious. It would be impossible for me to convince him. However, one question bothered me the whole way back: Had Vic just come along there by accident?

He helped me to get out of the car, I was in a pitiful state. I said a simple "Thanks" by way of a goodbye.

"I must take you back up to your apartment, Lilly. Give me your keys, please."

"You must? What do you mean?"

"Darren asked to me to," he said, looking downwards.

"What? I must have missed something there. What's he playing at?"

"I don't know, Lilly. He just explained where to find you, and asked me to take you back to your home. Right inside."

My look at this point was so inquisitive that it diverted his own. Then, he held his hand out for the keys.

Why had Darren become so protective after this night? What did he want, in the end? To help me or not?

Vic didn't know what to say, he seemed very embarrassed by the situation. I didn't know what Darren had told him. Could Vic be a vampire, too? I didn't ask him the question, I'd had my dose of vampirism for a while.

My perception of things had now changed, my plan was completely crazy and dangerous. Why hadn't I felt it before? I'd lived through the most terrible night of my existence. I'd never been so frightened. But this new development: I'd provoked it myself and I now knew I could never physically go through it again. I was exhausted, emptied. And yet, he'd hardly touched me. My life was too important to put at risk. I was just a fool in search of a better life, but I'd have to be content with what I had.

I started crying again on the stairs. The disappointment now, on top of everything else, had got to me, it was all too much. He opened the door. This was the first time a stranger had come into my home. I went straight to the bathroom, to run myself a bath. I slid into the very hot water, it felt great. Little by little, my breathing became normal once again.

I was trying to keep my eyes open, when suddenly Vic called out to me. He seemed worried.

"Are you ok, Lilly?"

"Yes, I'm getting out of the bath. You can leave, if you want. I'm feeling better."

"If it doesn't bother you, I'd rather wait a little."

"As you wish. Thanks, Vic."

I left the bathroom. The bath had done me good, but I still couldn't forget Darren's look. So close, so black, so evil! I shuddered even to think of it.

Sitting at the table, Vic was browsing through my book. I settled down in front of him and looked at him. I still wondered if, he too, was a vampire.

"Darren suggested that this book was utter nonsense. What do you think?"

"Must we believe in vampires, Lilly?"

His look was just like Darren's, at the club when he was angry. I kept my answer to myself. I played it safe.

"I don't know, Vic."

"You should go to bed."

"Yes, you're right. Thanks for your help, really. Just pull the door behind you as you leave."

"Sleep well!"

"Thanks. You too."

I went to bed hoping for a long and restorative night.

* * *

I'd stayed shut in at home for a week, I didn't even answer the telephone. Vic had phoned every day. I'd not even reopened the book, which I'd put on a shelf, far out of sight. I didn't dare leave my home. But, I needed to eat and my cupboards were empty.

Today, I walked around the aisles of my minimarket, not knowing what to get. I'd lost my appetite for anything. I was in a state of shock, I realised. Now that I was outside, every noise made me jump. Every scream reminded me how Darren had stifled mine. I looked around just about everywhere. I was feeling bad, very bad. Worse, I had no idea how to bring myself out of it! Nobody could help me, I had nobody to confide in. I was in a very dark impasse. I managed however to fill two shopping bags - mainly with fruit and dairy items - and hurry back home.

Vic was standing in front of the door to my building. As I came closer, his smile softened. He rushed to take the bags from my hands, as I was about to collapse. I'd over-estimated my fortitude. Just then, my strength abandoned me altogether.

I regained consciousness in my apartment. I was lying on the sofa, Vic was putting away my shopping. I tried to get up, but my head hurt badly.

"Don't move, you fell and hit your head badly. Luckily, I saved your shopping! If you tell me where I can find some ice and a towel, I'll make you a compress."

"The freezer for the ice; the top drawer in the bathroom for the rest. You've saved me once again?"

"Your meal more like, so it seems to me!"

He came to sit near me and delicately applied the ice to my forehead.

"Ouch!"

"If you didn't want to be hurt, you shouldn't fall. My mother kept telling me non-stop, when I was a child. Why didn't you answer the telephone? We were worried, you know."

"Who's "we"?"

"You know very well who."

He got up to make me something to eat. He carried on talking to me from the kitchen.

"What's the matter, Lilly? You can tell me all about it, I'm your friend. In any case, you are to me," he concluded, putting his head around the door, holding a carrot.

"You are to me as well."

I smiled at him. I really meant it, I liked him very much.

"In that case, why don't you answer when a friend calls you?"

"I don't know, I wanted to keep myself to myself."

"To the point of dying of hunger!"

"No. After what happened the other evening, I needed to reflect. I still don't understand."

"Life doesn't always bring us what we want from it, alas! Certain things can't be understood. There aren't explanations for everything, believe me."

I got up. I wanted to see his face while he was talking to me. I leaned against the kitchen door, the ice still on my forehead.

"I'm well placed to know that life doesn't always go the way we'd like. In my case specifically, there's an explanation. Pretending it's not so won't change anything. I have to overcome it, that's all. In any case, I can't ever forget it."

"You should face your fear, Lilly."

He was serious. I daren't try to understand.

"What do you mean?"

"Avoiding Darren isn't the solution."

I didn't have an answer. What should I do? Be insistent, to the point that he kills me? I didn't know whether Vic was talking on behalf of Darren. Did he know exactly what had happened? Did he think we'd had a simple quarrel? I ventured on:

"What did Darren tell you about the other evening?"

"Nothing. Only that I should take you home, if you were still there. That he'd maybe done a stupid thing. But, don't tell him I told you this, please."

I needed to sit down. Why was Darren worried about me? It was insane, completely illogical. His own words came back to me: "Drop it". Yet him, he hadn't dropped it. Now for sure, I was utterly confused. And Vic took so much care of me! Did Darren regret his actions, his intimidation, such that he sent me a guardian angel? I no longer knew what to think. I reassured Vic with a deliberate smile:

"Don't worry, I know how to keep a secret."

Vic wasn't to blame. If I wanted to bear a grudge against somebody, it should be Darren.

"You're going to eat the feast that I'm preparing you. Then, we'll go to the club, okay?"

"No, I'll savour your feast, but I'll stay here. I'm too feeble to go out, as you well saw."

"Balderdash!"

"What? Where did you come up with that word?"

"Well, from my vocabulary," he said, smiling.

"Nobody uses it these days."

"Really? Hey! Well I still do. Sit down, it's ready."

I obeyed without batting an eyelid, it smelt really good. In fact, the meal turned out to be delicious and I revelled in trying to find an excuse not to accompany him to the club. I didn't want to face Darren. It was too soon, I wasn't ready.

"It's exquisite! Where did you learn to cook?"

"My mother. It was my mother who taught me."

His lie was monumental, I didn't pursue it further.

One hour later, we were in front of the club. I was more than worried, I hadn't found an excuse which held good. This time, there was no going back.

He pushed me gently inside. The concert had begun, Marie had replaced Vic at the bar. I held back, watching Darren on the stage. I was scared, very scared. From now on, this place was no longer reassuring for me, he'd spoilt everything! And what if all this was only a trap?

So, I turned around, I pushed the door and I ran away. I ran along the middle of the road. I made a taxi stop dead in front of me. I hurriedly jumped inside. When I got home, I double-locked myself in. I hadn't been ready, I did warn him! I set my phone to silent and lay down, trembling all over.

I didn't manage to sleep. At one point, while turning over, I saw my answering machine blinking. I got up and erased the message without listening to it. Too bad if it was my mother, which I doubted.

Two weeks passed. Little by little, I recovered my spirit and my energy. I didn't go out much, but every attempt was a success. I got rid of my compulsion to look around all the time.

It was still very good weather for the month of October. Nevertheless, in spite of the mildness of the evenings, I avoided going out after nightfall. This ordeal had reinforced my taste for life. I tried to accept the conditions of my life, but it was hard. The alternative which I believed I'd found turned out to be too dangerous. With hindsight, I realised that I'd come very close to something irreversible and extremely grave.

I didn't know why it had ended this way. I loathed things left unfinished, I liked finding an answer for everything. My rational side, probably. So, unconsciously, for that reason my steps took me back in front of the club.

Something must have happened there, because wooden boards replaced the windows. I now understood Vic's silence for the last two weeks.

The doors were wide open, work was going on there. I ventured closer. On one of the wooden panels, a poster stated that the club was closed because of fire. My God, fire! I'd read in my book that fire was the only sure way to definitely eliminate a vampire. Those who'd done this knew it. Unless it was just accidental? Why always look for the dramatic side of things?

Out of curiosity, I poked my nose inside. Some workers cleared rubble, others stretched protective tarpaulins over the little which was still intact. Vic sat at a table stacked with papers, Darren a little farther away. Seeing him was a shock for me, it reminded me of our encounter at the Place des Vosges. But this time, I had nothing to be afraid of: The club was full of strangers, probably humans like me. At least, I hoped so.

"Hello Lilly," shouted Vic.

He got up and came over to meet me. He was beaming with friendship and seemed genuinely happy to see me, as I was to see him.

"Hello Vic, what happened?"

"A fire, Lilly. It was terrible. Fortunately, the club wasn't open at the time."

"Nobody was hurt?"

"No, not seriously at least. You'll come and sit down?"

"I'm not certain that's a good idea, he didn't even say hello to me."

"He's on the telephone, Lilly. Come on!"

He took my hand and offered me a seat. I felt uneasy, but not as much as I was afraid I'd be. I was getting better; a more than positive point.

I looked discreetly at Darren out of the corner of my eye, like the first time I'd come here. As a human, he was very beautiful. I didn't understand how I could be having such thoughts after what he'd done to me. I looked away, Vic had dived back into his papers.

The club was black with soot, it was everywhere. The restoration work would doubtless take quite some while.

"Hello Lilly," said Darren, hanging up at last.

His voice was normal. It was soft and pleasant. How could he be so different? I could no longer perceive any of his hatred from that night. I answered him, looking right into his eyes.

"Hello Darren"

"It's been a long time since you were here."

"I know. I needed to rest, to think. I'd been mistaken about many things. You were right, I'm afraid. Bad news for me. But certain things are too hard to bear. At least, they are for me. I over-estimated myself."

"Is there anything that I can do for you?" He asked as naturally as anything, as if nothing had happened.

I looked at him, bewildered, then almost screaming I said:

"I beg your pardon? It was clear you didn't want to help me. So, why make such an offer now?"

Vic found an excuse to get up. Since I started to become afraid, I also got up, but Darren put his hand on my arm. Apparently, the conversation wasn't finished. I sat back down, trying to stay calm.

"You won't avoid me for eternity, Lilly? I'm not going to hurt you. Speak to me."

"I don't understand you, and you, you offer nothing to enlighten me. You're suddenly quite different!"

He smiled at me.

"I said something funny?"

"No. According to you, I ought to have trusted you blindly. Look around you: Evil is everywhere, Lilly. Consider this: You appear in my life, you ask something of me... Yes, just unimaginable... And I'm supposed have said yes without knowing you, just because you demanded it?"

I lowered my eyes.

"You're right. Nevertheless, I trusted you one hundred percent. I told you everything, I was sincere."

"Now, I know this, yes. But admit it, that wasn't very prudent of you. I can't even dare to imagine what would've happened if you'd come across the ones who did this to the club. They would've transformed you, yes, but into a beast much worse than the one I showed you in that alley."

The fact that he could even mention it again gave me goose-bumps. I'll never forget that moment which, for him, only represented a test. He sensed it, because he placed his icy hand on my arm to reassure me. I sighed noisily.

"Did I pass the test successfully, Darren?"

This question undermined the last few days I'd spent chasing this crazy and dangerous idea out of my head. But I posed it all the same, without regard for the consequences.

"Yes."

"What am I to deduce from that?"

"Nothing for the moment. I still need to consider it. But promise me you'll be more careful in the future."

"I promise. But you, did you need to be so hard on me? To frighten me so much?"

I needed to know, I couldn't avoid posing him this question.

"It was necessary, yes. You were scared, but in reality, there wasn't anything to be frightened of: I stayed there the whole time, until Vic's arrival. We never took our eyes off you, Lilly. Never, believe me."

"Perhaps so, but psychologically, the shock was terrible, and that, it can't be dispelled. I shall never forget, Darren. I've just lived through some really very tough moments."

"I know and I do apologise. Will you forgive me one day?"

"Forgive? Honestly, I don't know. Forget? Never, I'm afraid."

On those words, I took my leave. Everything remained open to question. Once again, I went back home full of confusion, but strangely, I was now smiling. This conversation had done me good; but moreover, it gave me confidence. I'd given up too soon, there was still some hope. This time, I understood.

The following morning, I received a magnificent bouquet of flowers, with one simple word: "Try!"

3

The following Wednesday, I went back to the "Blood Blues Jazz Club". It'd been several days since Darren's words had resounded in my head. The more I kept going over them, the more I believed them. Was I finally going to get out of my nightmare?

He was there, sitting on the terrace. The sun set slowly over Paris, an autumnal sweetness displaced the heat wave of recent months. New windows had replaced wooden boards, the works were moving forward well.

He raised his head and our gazes met. My heart was racing as if this was a lovers' rendez-vous. And yet, this was a long way from being one. He came over to meet me and took me in his arms. His body, while cold, radiated an unexpected, almost agreeable warmth. His embrace surprised me; I was ready for anything, apart from this.

"Hello Lilly," he whispered.

I looked up towards him.

"Thanks for the flowers!"

"You're welcome, I owe you that at least. Lilly, listen to me… I can't promise you anything. I did some research and found not one word on the subject. In fact, I don't know if we have the faculty to cure humans at all."

"We can always try. You've got nothing to lose, you. Me, there's just my life. Even if it means getting another massive fright!"

"No. If we do it, there won't be anything to be afraid of, trust me. You know, a transformation rarely fails. But be aware of one thing: I don't know if it'll cure you. In which case, you would stay like this..."

"For all eternity," I murmured, realising that it would be the worst thing which could happen to me.

"Even worse than it is already…"

"I hadn't thought of that. Is there an alternative which can save me from this?"

"Would you be asking me to save you, and afterwards, if I fail, then to kill you purely and simply?"

"I couldn't live an eternity of hell. Understand me, Darren."

He took my head between his hands. Instinctively, I recoiled. He stared deeply into my eyes.

"Humans don't believe in us, some people even want to exterminate us. They're afraid of us. Us, the drinkers of blood, the killers of children! And you, you come to ask me to heal your life, to possibly even give it back it to you? Never has a human spoken to me as you do. Never has a human regarded me as a whole entity, when he learned what I was. So I'm not going to try anything for you without having the certainty that it'll work. Can you understand me?"

"Yes, but how will you know?"

"Give me your medical records, I need more details."

He sat back down at the table and invited me to do likewise. I lit a cigarette.

"Do you believe you can do something for me quickly?"

"Honestly, I really don't know. It could be sufficient for the moment to make you what I am," he said smiling, "but again I have to think about it. It's not a game, you know! As soon as we have all the facts to hand, we can make the final definitive decision. Together."

"As far as I'm concerned, it's already taken."

"You'll have to make me certain promises, and moreover, hold to them for all eternity. I can't allow myself any risk. I don't want to put my family in danger, even if the cause is vital."

"I understand. Will you tell me a little more about your life?"

"Upon your revival. Not before. Don't be so curious."

He got up and went into the bar. I didn't know what to do. Follow him? Stay here? Go back home?

A saxophone melody wafted its way over to me. Very soft; like a whisper. A murmur. In turn, I followed him. With a nod of his head, Vic pointed out the stage. This part of the club had now been restored, it was now very nice.

Darren was alone on the stage, there was no concert this evening. I sat down near him, on a high stool. He was playing with his eyes closed. What could he be thinking about? In turn, I too closed my eyes and began to hum this tune, which I knew, although the name escaped me.

"What song would you like me to play for you?"

"Of Jazz?"

"Not necessarily."

He smiled to me, he knew Jazz wasn't my cup of tea. But still I did want to fit in.

"Nora Jones, maybe...?"

"Good choice! What kind of music do you usually listen to?"

"A little bit of everything, from the instant that I feel the melody or the rhythm. It goes from Popular to Rock, passing through Metal, or even Classical. My feelings govern my choice. All the same, admittedly, I have a penchant for Gothic music. On the other hand, I hate Rap and Country!"

My musical tastes were rather eclectic. He smiled openly to me.

"If I play a piece which you know, would you sing for me?"

His question surprised me and made me blush.

"Oh! My God, no. I don't know how to sing…"

"You know how to hum very well… Singing shouldn't pose a problem. "My Immortal", does that work for you?"

"With the saxophone?"

"Of course not! I'm going to play the piano. Come and sit here."

He patted the seat near him.

"Hey! I'm not going to eat you!" He quipped.

He started playing the intro of one of my favourite songs. It was strange to hear it played just for me. He was as good on the piano as with the saxophone, better maybe, but it's true that my ear was more used to the piano.

I began to sing softly. My whole body was trembling. Stage fright, probably. I imagined that I was alone. I closed my eyes.

I'm so tired of being here
Suppressed by all of my childish fears
And if you have to leave
I wish that you would just leave
'Cause your presence still lingers here
And it won't leave me alone

As the melody progressed, the words came naturally back to me. How many times had I heard this song?

Subconsciously, I knew the words off by heart. I was watching the video clip in my head, this was a magical moment. I'd often dreamed of a moment such as this.

At the end of the piece, I took a few seconds to reopen my eyes.

"Hey! You never told us you could sing, Lilly!" Shouted Vic from the counter.

"Oh! I can't sing", I mumbled.

"Ah? What do you call that, then?"

"I was carried along with the music, I just followed the piano and I don't deserve any merit."

I smiled shyly, turning my head towards Darren, he seemed as emotional as I was.

"Thank you Darren, it was wonderful."

"Thanks to you, really magical! We have a lot to learn about each other, I believe."

This last sentence aroused so much hope! I prayed that he'd accept. Then, we'd have eternity to get to know each other.

I stood up. It was late and I was tired. It was one of those days which reminded me that I wasn't altogether like everybody else.

"I have to go home. Thanks again for this wonderful evening."

He looked at me with concern.

"Good evening, Lilly. You're a perfect musical partner. Don't forget the documents!"

"I'll send them to you by courier tomorrow, if that's okay?"

"Yes, that's great."

He got up and accompanied me back to the door. In the passage, I said goodbye to Vic who was talking with a customer over a cup of coffee.

"Would you like me to take you home in the car?"

"No thanks, the walk will do me good."

"You seem so tired, suddenly ..."

He frowned. I answered with a lie:

"It'll pass, I promise!"

He kissed my hand and watched me leaving. I felt his gaze upon me right up to the corner of the street. There, I risked a quick glance in his direction and I raised my hand by way of one last goodbye. He did the same.

* * *

I rested at home for the next three days. I must have caught a cold, because I was feverish. Impossible to put a foot out of the bed. Nevertheless, I'd sent my medical records to Darren, giving him plenty of time to study it. I hoped to get better this evening so I could return to the club.

All of a suddenly, someone banged on my door. Obviously, I'd fallen asleep again. Night had fallen. Damned fever!

I got up and slipped on my pullover to answer the door. Nobody knew my address, except Vic. I looked through the peephole: It was Darren.

"Lilly, open up, please!"

"Yes, if I can find my keys!"

Generally, I'd leave my keys in the door, but they weren't there. I found them finally in my coat. Darren bounded into the apartment, seemingly very worried.

"Are you all right?"

"Yes… I believe so, finally. I fell asleep again. I wanted to go to the club this evening, but in my opinion, it's too late."

"Do you know its Monday, Lilly?"

"Monday…?"

I tried to hide my concern. I'd never slept like that, without being aware of how much time had passed. Strange…

"You want a coffee, Darren?"

"Yes, it would be very welcome."

He refused sugar, but accepted milk. We sat at the kitchen table, in silence. I felt much better. The sleep had been long, but restorative.

"I studied your medical records, and showed them to a doctor friend. In theory, no problem, but it's a first: Vampires don't habitually study their intended "prey". As for knowing whether it will cure you of your human ills, nobody can predict."

"Have you made a decision?"

"I'm still thinking about it even at this moment. It's a big responsibility."

"I can sign you a discharge…"

He roared with laughter.

"What are you going to write on your discharge? "I Lilly, the undersigned, do swear not to pursue Darren in case of failure following my transformation into a vampire"?"

He leant towards me, very seriously, almost terrifyingly. I recoiled instinctively.

"You'll write nothing about this act, Lilly. On the contrary, you're going to make me some promises, which you must uphold if you don't want to lose your life."

"You frighten me."

I ought to have said "still", but I changed my mind.

"It has to be done, Lilly."

"What promises?"

"The first one: All this must remain secret. Nobody must know what I'm going to do for you, nor what will have happened. Nobody must know where to find us, not even your mother... Or worse still, your doctor. When do you have to see him again?"

"In December."

"Not a word, okay?"

"And if it works, I say what?"

"That it's a miracle. We'll take care of the details later. You must also promise me two more things: Be loyal towards me and above all, be a kind vampire."

"That's to say what?"

"Never betray me for another vampire! Now, pay great attention to what I am going to say: Never attack a human being and never drink the liquid blood of a human being."

I opened my eyes widely.

"You don't feed on blood?"

"Things have evolved, Lilly, I've already told you. You'll be a part of my family and you'll have to follow its rules. If you break them, you risk punishment, banishment, or worse still, death. Know that your life will be different; nothing will ever be as before..."

"Already nothing's as it was before. Okay... Am I going to suffer?"

I drank a mouthful of coffee to warm myself. He'd still not touched his, far too concentrated on his directives.

"No, I'm not violent, even if you think to the contrary. But for the sake of discretion, I'll bite you in the foot."

"The neck, is it a legend, then?" I said, laughing.

"No, it's the most uncovered place when we attack somebody by surprise. But we don't attack humans any more. Not in my family, in any case."

"Nevertheless, you did show me that you're always capable of it."

The image of the doorway came to mind, a shiver went right through me.

"Of course. Our instinct never leaves us, it's enough to know how to control it. What's more, there was a reason for this attack. Now, you know this. Try to forget, please."

"I'm trying desperately, Darren."

He was smiling at me and I understood that he accepted, in spite of the risks to himself. He quite simply trusted me, as I'd done with him, since the first day. A mutual trust. Darren must have been a nice person as a human being.

He left, from now on reassured about my state of health, and by my promise to be silent and especially to be loyal to him and his family.

I went back to bed, my head full of hope for a better life.

* * *

I came back inside having done some shopping, because my fridge was empty again. I felt better and I was as hungry as a wolf. I put the bags down on the kitchen table.

I began to tidy away my purchases, when I noticed my answering machine was blinking. I had a message.

"Lilly, come to the club on Friday at 8pm. Bring a bag and enough clothes for a few days, we're leaving for the weekend."

This simple sentence filled me with joy, but also with concern. We'd got there, I could no longer turn back. So, I decided to spend my last days as a human, by the sea.

I arrived in Honfleur in the early evening. This late in the season, I'd easily find a room facing the sea. I liked this city. A bit of a holiday atmosphere still persisted there, but it was very quiet all the same. Exactly what I needed. Having put away my meagre luggage, I decided to go for a walk on the seashore.

I sat down on a low wall, to contemplate the coastline while savouring a passion fruit ice cream. A lovely gentle breeze caressed my face, I cleared my head of everything.

I tried to grasp what I was about to do, it was however rather difficult. I tried to be rational, but what was the use? All of this was unimaginable. Nevertheless, I wanted it. Nothing could be worse than what I lived through day after day as a human being.

* * *

The following Friday, as agreed, I found myself with my bag in front of the club. My stomach was overcome with dread, I was terrified. I slowly pushed the door open. The club was half full. Some customers were drinking from their glasses and discussing the rain and the good weather still lingering at the beginning of autumn. I swept my gaze across the counter, the room and the stage, I didn't see Darren. Had he forgotten?

"Hello Lilly," Vic called out from the counter.

"Hello Vic."

My voice betrayed my anxiety. He invited me to sit down at the bar. Did he know what was going to take place this evening? Darren would be a little late; something unforeseen.

"A coffee?"

"Something a little stronger..."

"Are you okay?"

"Yes, I just need a little courage."

I was tense. I had only one impulse: To flee. But it wouldn't solve my problems. I had to stay, to be courageous for a better life. I'd wanted this, so I'd stay.

A few moments later, which to me seemed an eternity, Darren pushed open the door of the Club. A big smile lit up his face, he came to settle himself down near me.

"Hello Lilly, where did you spend these last few days?"

"In Honfleur, the sea relaxes me."

"Very good choice, I adore this region. But not in the summer: Too many humans."

He finished his sentence with a sarcastic whisper. He didn't seem to be under any stress.

"You didn't change your mind?"

"No. Look, I have my bag, I'm ready. At last, I believe it. I'm terrified."

He put his hand on my cheek, his gaze was gentle.

"You're frozen! Don't worry, it'll be all right."

"Okay, okay."

"From now on, I'll take care of everything. Just do what I ask of you. Don't ask questions and don't worry. You can trust me, right?"

"Yes, of course. I do however have one last question."

"Okay, but it's the last one!" He said jokingly.

He visibly tried to relax the atmosphere; a difficult thing, considering my stressed state.

"If the vampires in your family don't drink blood any longer, how can you do this?"

"Very good question! I'm not going to drink your blood Lilly, or only a little, at the time of the bite. I wouldn't be able to avoid that. Vampires which are drinkers of blood kill human beings or animals by emptying them of their blood; here, it's not the aim. During this transformation, it's me who's going to pass something on to you, I'm going to inject my venom into your blood. You understand the difference?"

"Yes, but this venom, isn't it toxic?"

"Of course it is. If this wasn't the case, no transformation would be possible."

"In films, we see the victims writhing in pain."

He smiled mockingly.

"They are films, Lilly. We're going to stop the questions, because the more you want to know about it, the more you're going to worry. And yet, I think you're already worried enough."

"You're right, forgive me."

"Shall we go?"

"Where are we going?"

"We did say: No more questions!"

He got up smiling, took my bag, took me by the hand and invited me to follow him. The clammy touch of his cold hand against mine, froze my blood. I'd soon feel faint, I sensed it.

We left in the car to meet my fate, towards my new life. I prayed to God that it would be only better. But God, could he help me in this quest?

4

A sunbeam infiltrated through the chink in the curtains which I'd left open the day before. Instinctively, my hand settled on my foot. No, I'd not dreamed it: The wound was very much there. Principally, it had healed. The pain had disappeared. A positive point.

As Darren had predicted, the night had helped me recover my memory. Everything was clear, now: I was alive. A single question remained, but the answer would only be known after some time. The transformation was a partial success, even if the second phase hadn't taken place. I'd not asked any questions about "afterwards". It was too late now, anyway.

A dressing-gown had been placed on the bed. I slipped it over my pullover and headed over to the window to admire the park. The daylight didn't disturb me in the least. Another legend, probably.

The door was no longer locked and I ventured onto the balcony, or rather the terrace. I hadn't noticed this detail yesterday evening.

A fresh wind blew on my face and in my hair. Yes, I was alive! I began to descend the stone steps which led to the park. I felt good and on discovering the space around me, I smiled. My God, how big it was! No… Grandiose!

If I hadn't known about what'd happened, I would've imagined it was a fairy tale or a day-dream. Who doesn't dream of waking up in a big four-poster bed? Of walking in a French garden with, in the background, a luxurious chateau?

As for me, this chateau: I'd not previously come across it. I'd imagined this place to have been derelict for centuries.

I sat down on a low wall surrounded with rosebushes, in front of the building. The view was magnificent and I felt no desire for food, to drink or even to smoke. My transformation had at least that going for it!

I was scrutinising the facade of this immense building, when I became aware of him on the steps. He waved to me, then came over. I didn't really know the attitude to adopt. I watched him approach with an assured walk. He was even more beautiful today. The wind played with his long hair, which seemed to annoy him a little. With a refined motion, he gathered his plentiful hair aside and kept it imprisoned in his hand.

He hadn't stopped smiling since I'd seen him on the steps. My acuteness of vision had changed, I persuaded myself. He shone.

"Hello Lilly."

"Hello Darren. The door was open, I came outside…"

"You've done well. My doctor friend is coming over for the morning."

"I feel different."

"And so you are. Let's say that your transformation was surprising in its simplicity and calmness. In general, this takes place somewhat differently. I can't tell you any more now, let's wait until he examines you. Okay?"

He delicately tilted my face upwards, tears flowed down my cheeks. I couldn't keep myself from thinking that my transformation had failed. I felt very different, but still human. My tears were then transformed into a torrent which I couldn't hold back.

Spasms suddenly shook my whole body. I was worried, I implored Darren:

"What's happening? I can feel my lucidity abandoning me... My God, I'm in such pain!"

"Come down from that wall, please."

He laid me out on the ground. I was terrified. I heard him shouting to Hector to call the doctor as quickly as possible. My eyes rolled backwards, every muscle in my body was seized up, I felt the pain of death. But I was still conscious: I was living through my transformation after the event, since everything had seemed finished!

He was on his knees behind me and kept my head securely between his legs. My body had become a free entity, which raised itself, reared up and tried to escape from Darren's steady embrace. I began to scream, my tears descended into an inhuman rage. I held my hands to my face, even the slightest centimetre of skin burned. I had only one urge: To tear it away from me. Then, suddenly, I stared at my hands in terror. My skin was translucent, I saw the blood navigating its way at top speed in my veins. A figure approached and squatted with us. I observed him in the way an animal would, turning my head from right to left, ready to pounce.

I had the impression that my eyes had left my body: I was capable of seeing the scene from above, which frightened me even more! My God, what had I done? It seems that the dying see themselves from above before walking towards the light. So was I now dying?

What I saw was deeply moving; stretched out on the ground, a being writhing in pain. By her side, two men looked at her and waited for it all to finish. Her face was deformed by the spasms, her skin was almost transparent, she was sweating, her hair stuck to her cheeks. Little by little she stopped crying, she implored that her ordeal would come to an end. Her eyes took on an indefinable colour and, in a last surge, like a final deliverance, she fell again serenely on the ground.

"Martin, I believe that we have our answer," announced Darren with relief.

"Effectively, but this two-stage transformation leaves me sceptical..."

Martin was the doctor for the vampire community. He was highly respected, and also very old. I learned afterwards that he was French and was 450 years old, although he seemed barely to be fifty.

Darren picked me up in his arms and brought me back to my bedroom. I was half conscious. I felt the balance of his steps, so soft after so much violence. Calmed now, I slowly reopened my eyes. My head lost itself in his hair, I felt his skin, I smelt it... And suddenly, it started again... My hands tightened around his head, I noticed my nails lengthen, the heat of his body intoxicated me. Then, in a lightning flash, I planted my teeth into his neck, drinking in his blood, and its heat filled me up.

He didn't react. He was quite passive whilst also quickening his step to my room.

"That's enough, now," he said, lying me on the bed.

He tore me away me from him. What had come over me?

Martin approached me, whereas Darren dried his neck.

"Welcome into our world, Miss Lilly. I'm Martin, the family's doctor. I had come to see why you hadn't completed your transformation, but at this moment, I believe it's all done!"

It mattered not what Martin said, I looked around for Darren.

"My God, I hurt him!"

Martin put his hands on my shoulders.

"No, Lilly, you ended the process."

He was trying to be reassuring, but in vain. I was horrified by what I'd done.

"He'd told me never to bite a human being."

"But I'm not human, Lilly. Calm yourself down, what you did was normal. Now, I can guarantee that you are transformed one hundred percent. You even have a good bite!"

He smiled, massaging his neck. Not a single trace of my bite now remained. He didn't seem angry. I should've asked more questions beforehand. Or at least, I should have tried.

I looked at them both. I was deathly pale. An irresistible urge to vomit came over me. I could see myself biting him again, planting my teeth into his flesh. What a strange feeling! Right now, I, too, was a vampire.

"Are you okay, Lilly?" asked Martin.

"Yes, I just feel a little sick. I'm so sorry for my action! I don't know if I'll find a way to make you forgive me."

"Lilly, listen to me…"

Sitting on the edge of the bed, Darren looked straight into my eyes. The fear rose inside me again.

"Normally, a transformation doesn't take place like this. For a "normal" human being, in less than an hour, the process is complete. And what's more, seeing the speed of events, the person holds few memories of it. You lived it across two days; you maybe even vaguely remember my bite."

"No, not at all… Not yours, in any case."

I made myself feel guilty.

"Lilly, stop it! All this is normal. What isn't, is that you lived consciously through the end of the transformation."

"I'd been so well in the garden! I told myself that after all, it wasn't so terrible…"

This time, I was close to tears.

"Lilly, it's unusual, but you knew it could be different for you. In any case, everything is different with you; and now in both worlds, apparently!"

"You didn't want to explain to me what would happen… From then on"

"What would you have done, if you'd known? Would you have given up?"

"No."

"In that case, I don't see the point of knowing any more about it. What's more, you would've taken me for a liar. I prefer that things happened the way they did."

"Maybe you're right."

He took my head between his hands. His look was piercing, as blue as the bottom of the ocean.

"Martin is going to try to understand what may have changed the situation. But tell yourself that it's well and truly ended: You're a vampire, you have to accept it and live with the memory of your transformation. If you have any doubt, think this: "I'm well, I knew it would take place like that, I wasn't surprised, I didn't suffer, and look… There's no trace of it"."

He finished his sentence with a smile.

"All right. So it's really ended?"

"Yes, I promise."

He kissed me on the forehead, his skin was no longer ice-cold. He pulled me delicately up to him with a warm embrace, and whispered:

"All's well, Lilly. Believe me, would you?"

"I believe you."

This contact surprised me. Nothing to do with what I'd felt at the club terrace. There, something was different: Me!

They both left the room, I had to rest. After so many emotions, a little solitude would do me a world of good. It was like after a surgical operation: Upon awakening, we're always a little bit worried about the result; then, as the anaesthetic wears off, as our mind becomes clearer, we smile at the idea of still being alive despite the all the risks.

I was alive and that was the main thing. I'd arrived at my goal. Let's hope the future would prove me right!

5

A few hours later, the urge came to take a shower. I got up and headed to a door situated at the far end of the bedroom. My instinct proved me right: It was indeed the bathroom. I was a little surprised by its modernity, because the contrast with the bedroom was flagrant. Even vampires knew how to keep up with contemporary taste!

A big quarter-circle bathtub took pride of place in the middle of the room. It was surrounded with fine white curtains which fluttered in a gentle breeze. It was magical!

Behind a folding screen, I discovered a window. I approached it carefully, because I still didn't know what effect the sun would produce on my skin, since it had become so white.

I ran the water and scattered some blue salts I'd found on a white satin-covered stool into the bottom of the bath. The water was tepid, bluish like the ocean. I slowly submerged my body. A feeling of peace overcame me, the scars on my foot had now vanished. Then I looked through the window. The wind had risen at the same time as the sun, the trees were bent over by its gusts. It was beautiful, everything seemed beautiful to me. This restored optimism was new.

Suddenly, a ludicrous idea occurred to me: If I was a vampire, I could therefore do things which human beings were incapable of? I allowed myself to slide to the bottom of the bathtub and began to count, with my eyes wide open. Reaching one hundred, I realised I hadn't run out of air; by two hundred, I was smiling. I experienced no discomfort at all. For me, who adored water, this new ability filled me with untold joy.

The more the water cooled, the more I felt good there. That also, that was new. Previously, I would've been incapable of having a tepid bath, and even less so a cold one. I'd no idea for how long I'd lounged in the water, I'd lost my track of time a little.

Another question suddenly occurred to me: how was I going to dress? I reluctantly left my ice-cold ocean, and went off to explore the wardrobes in the bedroom.

I wasn't at all surprised to find my clothes there, folded and arranged. So I slipped on my jeans and my favourite pullover, the black polo-necked one. I was ready now for the events which would follow. I gathered up my wet hair and fastened it on top of my head using a clip I'd found on the bedside table.

The door wasn't locked, but it creaked a little. The tour of the premises could begin. What would I discover inside this chateau?

My bedroom was situated at the end of a long corridor scattered with numerous doors, all quite identical, between which paintings were hung. These depicted landscapes, all in different periods. I was incapable of pinpointing which, but I now had eternity ahead of me. This thought rendered me serene: I had time, the whole of time!

The far end of my corridor constituted the beginning of three others: North, west and east. The corridors to the west and east were identical to mine: Nothing but perfectly identical doors. I ought instead perhaps to take bearings if I'd want to find my room again in this labyrinth!

I chose the corridor to the north, because the door at the far end drew my attention. Nevertheless, arriving in front of it, I hesitated to open it. I didn't want to be indiscreet. So I knocked gently, waiting for an answer which didn't come. I took the option of entering.

The spectacle which offered itself before me took my breath away. In all of my life, I'd never imagined a room such as this one. My dream! It was octagon-shaped and every wall was filled with books. There were hundreds. No, thousands! The ceiling was very high, a ladder on castors was leaning against the first column of books, just on my left. The shelves were never-ending. On my right, a window allowed a shaft of sunlight to penetrate; the wooden shutters were half-open.

I closed the door and began to observe the books. A strong smell of wood and paper filled the room and my body. My sense of smell had become extremely well developed. I'd never smelt books in this way, it was more than delightful. Then, suddenly, I smelt another odour. Familiar, this one. All my senses were stirred. I was on the alert. A person who I knew was somewhere nearby. I didn't know exactly where, but it was close enough for me to smell them.

"Hello, Lilly."

I jumped, and turned around. The character hadn't appeared where I'd expected. I let out a yell of fright.

"Hello, Darren."

"Did I scare you?"

"A little... Where the devil did you come in?"

"Here," he answered calmly.

He pointed out a secret door behind him; he seemed highly amused at the situation.

"Of course," I said, shaking my head.

"You like my library?"

"No..."

I paused for a moment and then I resumed:

"I love it! This place is wonderful."

"I am rather proud of it. I've maintained it through the years."

He punctuated his sentence with a wink.

"You should be proud of it. I haven't had time to look around yet, but the way this room is arranged pleases me very much. I've always dreamed about finding myself in a place such as this."

"It exactly fulfils its purpose. When I'm in need of peace, I come here. I could spend hours here. Without reading, besides!"

"Was this room forbidden to me?"

"No, you're a part of my family, now. Nothing here is a secret for you anymore. Just try to put every item back in its place. Hector is very fastidious."

"Who is Hector? Why is he always here?"

"He's my butler. But it's his own choice. It's a long story; he feels indebted to me."

"He shouldn't feel so?"

"As I told you, it's his choice."

"There are still some secrets, it seems..."

"All in good time, Lilly. So, tell me: What did you do this morning?"

"I had a lukewarm bath. I drowned myself, but I survived. I found my clothes and then I ventured up here."

"Drowned? You look very much alive for someone who drowned!"

"I know. Since I'm a vampire, apparently, water can no longer kill me."

"It is one of our advantages."

He adopted a much more serious tone and continued:

"Anyway, be careful with your experiments!"

"In that case, you'll have to tell me a little more, so I don't go too far."

"What would you like to know? But wait, let's sit down, that way we'll be better able to discuss it."

"Where?"

"Come, follow me!"

We took the little secret door from the library and we emerged into a monumental room. A fire crackled in the fireplace. Two very spacious armchairs faced each other. He invited me to sit in the one on the left.

"Would you like something to drink?"

"I can drink?"

"Why wouldn't you be able to? We drank at the club, you'll remember."

"That's true."

Hector was here already, waiting for our choices.

"What would you like, Lilly?"

"A hot milk?"

"If you want. For me, it'll be a cappuccino, Hector."

"I'd always read that vampires didn't drink and didn't feed themselves either..."

"We drink, but we don't feed ourselves. At least, not as humans do. Blood is essential to our survival. It is liquid. So, for this very reason, we can drink. As for food, a little later on, I shall invite you to share my feast. You've tasted some already, do you no longer remember it?"

- 75 -

"Apart from the soup which Hector brought me yesterday, I don't remember anything else."

"You'll see," he said with a note of amusement.

Hector brought our hot drinks straight away, which he put down on the coffee table between our armchairs. He was very discreet and it delayed me finding out about his history. What had Darren done that this man felt obliged to stay in his service for all eternity?

"Good! I'm ready to answer your questions. Your apprenticeship can begin, Lilly."

He smiled at me. Actually he smiled almost all of the time, except yesterday, in front of that low wall, but he was worried about of the turn of events. And of course, in the famous alley... Today, he was just as I'd otherwise known him: Reassuring, thoughtful, full of kindness and more inclined to answer questions.

"Why couldn't I drown myself?"

"It's not a means of killing a vampire. Our bodies have adapted to water. Living and breathing underwater even gives us quite a pleasant sensation, but there's a limit not to be exceeded, and I'll ask you to watch out for it, because you wouldn't realise your distress. Did you find it pleasant, this morning?"

"Yes, very. And the sun?"

I was impatient for any knowledge.

"The sun is no longer an enemy for vampires. Nor the daylight, as you may have observed. However, we have to avoid high temperatures, our bodies don't like it. We dehydrate faster than a human being. Never get lost in a desert and don't try to get a tan either!"

"Is that because our skin is so white?"

"Partly, but also because of our blood itself and its composition. This changes the pigmentation of our skin."

"Can I go back to walking in the park?"

"Of course! And even farther. It's going to be necessary for me to introduce you to the family."

"I know certain members already?"

"Yes, the group at the club: Vic, the barman, my sister Marie and Martin. But there are others. For the moment, only Martin and Hector are aware of your transformation. We no longer transform human beings since we don't bite them anymore. At least, in our family. I'm going to have to explain to them why I did it, upon your request. They will take you for a madwoman, and I; for a reckless fool. This game isn't yet won..."

I was worried by what he'd just said.

"Is it dangerous for you?"

"Although "father" of the family, I ought to have asked for their advice, or at least to have informed them. They could banish me for this, but I took the risk."

"Why?"

"For you. Your story has made me... How shall I say...? Fond of you. I didn't feel any danger from you, nor any manipulation. You were sincere and felt completely drained. Equally I felt that something might very soon happen to you. That's the reason I came to your home when we didn't hear any news from you. I was already very worried."

"What could happen to me?"

"I don't have the gift of clairvoyance, but I sensed a danger."

"Do you still feel it?"

"No, I'm very serene about that side of things."

"Thank God! Regarding senses, my sense of smell has improved considerably, right?"

"Yes, but in a very different way. Didn't you smell me in the library?"

"Yes! I smelt somebody. I didn't know who, but I was on the alert."

"You can only smell vampires. Humans don't release this hormone which we possess. It's a means of recognition that can prove to be useful."

"I also smelt the books, the ink, the wood."

"In fact, all scents are multiplied tenfold. The good as well as the bad. Sometimes, I would prefer not to have this gift!"

I smiled to him. I was like a child. Millions of questions occurred to me.

"My eyes also have changed."

"Your whole body changed. Your senses improved. Fortunately so, since we need them for our survival."

He concluded his sentence with a big smile at the precise moment when Hector entered the room to clear away our cups.

"It is 3 o'clock, Sir."

"Yes. Thanks Hector."

"Do you still have need of me?"

"No, you can join Amélie. Thank you."

On those words, Darren got up. I did the same and thanked Hector at the same time. It was the first time I'd seen a smile on his face. A question was nagging me:

"Who is Amélie?"

"His wife. They live in the house located at the entrance of the park. We'll maybe see them when we leave, they spend their time gardening. She adores plants."

"Where are we going? Do I need to change?"

"No, you're perfect. We're going to the club. This evening, we're giving a concert for a human friend of Vic's. It's its birthday."

"Good…"

The matter of leaving the chateau worried me a little, but that idea excited me. We took his car.

The park was never-ending, it was far beyond what I'd imagined. This property was immense. How could Hector maintain it all on his own? Unless the gardens were taken care of by Amélie?

My new life enthralled me: So many questions without answers, so many things to be discovered! Passing the gate, I didn't notice either Hector or his wife. Just a golden retriever seemed to be standing guard in front of the house.

The chateau was situated to the West of Paris, the area which I knew the least. It was thus difficult to place myself. The motorway was several kilometres away. We took this route heading towards the capital.

"How long before we reach the club?"

"It'll depend on the traffic. At this time, I'd say a good two hours. There are some Cd's in the glove compartment, if you'd like."

Darren seemed barely inclined to talk. He seemed preoccupied. It is true that we were going to meet members of the family, they were going to sense my transformation and this evening perhaps wouldn't be as relaxing as I'd imagined. My choice alighted on a 'Live' album, it was surprising to find one here. I slotted it into the player and watched the scenery streaming by.

Darren drove quickly, but not excessively so. I felt safe, which wasn't always the case when travelling by car. On the other hand, I didn't dare to break the silence he'd imposed. So I closed my eyes, carried away by the music and the speed, but I perked up suddenly.

"What day is it today?"

"October the 31st, the day of Halloween. Why?"

"I should be back at work on December the 10th."

"You have strange thoughts, sometimes."

"Yes, I know, but I mustn't forget. For others, I do still exist and I have obligations."

"Indeed."

We arrived at the outskirts of Paris. The traffic became heavier and I left Darren to concentrate on the road. A lot of suburbanites were on their way home, traffic jams started to form. The closer we came to the club, the more I sensed Darren was preoccupied, but I didn't dare disturb him.

He knew Paris well. We avoided the main roads, he took the side streets. During a stop at a red light, I half-opened my window and so understood the significance of his words: "All scents are multiplied tenfold" … I was overcome by all the smells around me. I was overtaken with nausea. I closed the window right away. Darren smiled at my misfortune, I'd managed to relax him without saying a word.

"Here we are," he said.

I got ready to get out of the car, when he put his hand firmly on my arm. I turned to him.

"Lilly, listen to me."

He seemed really worried.

"Don't say anything, let me bring up your transformation myself. If anyone tries to lead you into this conversation, avoid it."

"I'll do my best, I promise."

"Don't underestimate them, Lilly. And be wary of Marie!"

"Okay."

His concern was so intense, it pervaded me too.

"Let's go, stay near me for the moment."

He pushed open the door to the Club. The smell was new and strong, nothing like it had been at the red light. This one didn't give me nausea, it comforted me.

"Good evening everybody," he shouted.

Under the circumstances, I could have imagined a more discreet entrance. Clinging to him, I smiled timidly. He held his hand out to me, turned towards me and said:

"Do you remember Lilly?"

"Of course!" Vic called out from his counter.

They came up to me to be formally introduced. Some smiled, others less so. This entrance with its fanfare was without doubt a part of Darren's plan. In any case, one thing was for sure right now: They knew that I was here!

Marie didn't come over to me, she seemed to sulk in her corner. The introductions over, each returned to their glass and to their conversation, which had been interrupted by our arrival.

"Come, let's go and greet Marie," he said, taking my hand again.

"Shouldn't we have shown ourselves here discreetly?"

"It wasn't the best solution. Now, they know you. It won't prevent the questions, but now it's to me that they'll put them. Without that introduction, they would've addressed you."

"All right."

"Hello Marie, do you remember Lilly?"

"Yes, but she was different, the previous time. Or am I wrong?"

Her look was black, icy, she frightened me. Why her and not the others? What was the difference with her, apart from being Darren's sister? But basically, was she even truly his sister? At least, his sister in the "human" sense?

I held my hand out to her. She got up, came over to me and took me in her arms. A strange, uncomfortable embrace. She smelled me; this situation was very embarrassing. I freed myself as politely as possible and stepped back a pace. Silence descended around us. She broke it coolly:

"Hello Lilly, welcome among us!"

"Thank you Marie."

She sat back down again, the conversations started once more. This woman possessed an undeniable power. She took herself across to her brother. Her voice expressed a mixture of both anger and concern.

"What have you done, Darren? It's against our laws."

"This is different, believe me. You trust me, no?"

He spoke to her in a low voice, very calmly, like an elder brother wanting to reason with his little sister. She didn't stop being angry.

"Martin knows about this?"

"Of course! I consulted him and I obtained his approval."

"Maybe, but it's from the Clan you should have solicited approval. Were you afraid we would have refused it to you? In what way is this different? What's so special about her?"

In her look, only anger now remained, almost hatred. Was she jealous at not having been taken into confidence?

A "Happy birthday, Pierre!" fortunately cut short the conversation. The star of the evening made his entrance into the Club.

"We'll talk about it again later, Marie. It's neither the place nor the time for it. Be kind with her, please."

"Since you've asked to me to, for you, I shall be," she answered begrudgingly.

This last phrase was far from reassuring. We immediately went over to the group which had formed around Pierre. Was he aware that he was surrounded mainly by vampires? Probably. I supposed that lots of humans were in the know, but kept silent. Due to the physical changes which vampires had undergone over the course of the centuries, it was difficult to differentiate them at first sight from a human. Nowadays, lots of people had very pale skin, and without very close contact, the difference wasn't obvious. Now I had to become accepted into the family of vampires, the family which had now become mine. I hoped that they would allow me in.

"Don't worry about Marie."

A voice whispered those words behind me. I turned around: It was a member of Darren's group.

"Hello, I'm Henry, the double bassist in the group. We met a long time ago."

"Yes, I remember, hello. Why should I be worried about her?"

"She's a little, let's say… Emotional, demonstrative, theatrical. But in fact, she's very kind."

"All right, thank you. Who is Pierre?"

Pierre was busy unwrapping his presents. They were everywhere, all over the counter, and a bigger one placed on the floor. He seemed delighted and really very much at ease. He knew everybody, except for me, of course.

"Pierre is a very old friend of Vic's. A human. Vic saved him from a fire when he was little. All of his family died, so they're very close. We've celebrated his birthday here for thirty-two years. Funny, isn't it?"

"Yes. I suppose that he's aware…?"

"Not for a very long time, in fact. We told him when he asked us why he grew older, and not us. He was sixteen years old."

He finished his sentence in a roar of laughter. Yes, it's a question that lots of people would like to ask.

"How did he take it?"

"Calmly. I think he was at the best age. In adolescence, we believe everything we're told."

"You weren't afraid that he'd tell everyone around him?"

"No, we made him swear to keep it secret."

"And that was enough to reassure you?"

"Of course! He'd lost everything, we'd welcomed him into our family, we almost brought him up; why would he go telling stories about vampires? Who would have believed him, anyway?"

"I don't know."

I was surprised by such trust. I turned to Darren, I felt his gaze upon me.

"You're curious," he said, smiling.

"Yes, it interests me."

"We have to get up on the stage now, be careful."

He gave a hint of a smile, but I felt he was still worried.

"You coming, Henry?" He said, putting his hand on his friend's shoulder.

Henry and the rest of the group went to the stage. The other guests settled down in the room. Vic served drinks around the tables. I decided to stay in the bar like on the first day, far away from it all. It certainly wasn't the best way to join the family, but from here, the view was excellent.

"What can I get you, Lilly?" Vic asked me finally.

"A hot milk. It looks as if it's become my favourite drink."

"Here you are."

He put the cup down in front of me, along with two white capsules. I was perplexed...

"Why are you sitting here, on your own?"

"I have a beautiful view from here. And what's more, it's a family party. I wouldn't want to impose."

"You're a part of the family, from now on."

"Really?"

"What makes you think otherwise?"

"I don't know. I need to get used to it, and get to know all these people. You, I know you, so I feel safe."

He rewarded me with a big smile, then turned around to clean his glasses and to throw the gift wrapping in the litter bin. It's true that the counter was a little bit cluttered.

I was lost in my thoughts, I was feeling sad. Darren was right: The game wasn't won. I felt guilty for giving him so much cause for concern. I turned my head around to watch him playing. That very moment, I saw Marie heading over to me. Over her shoulder, I glimpsed Darren's look and I sensed his uneasiness. What a strange sensation it was to feel the emotions of others. Upon reflection, I realised that I could only do this with him. Was that because it was he who engendered me?

"How do you feel?" She asked from the outset.

"Honestly, not very comfortable."

"Hang on… You should have thought about that beforehand, my dear! I'm asking myself how you managed to convince my brother to transform you."

I looked at her, stunned by such aggressiveness. It was going be difficult to divert the conversation as Darren had asked me to do. Besides, she'd tackled me directly on the taboo subject.

"I don't believe it's up to me to speak to you about it, I'm sorry."

"Ah? And why not?"

"Because he asked me not to."

"He told you not to speak to me about your transformation?"

"No, he asked me not to speak to anybody about it."

It was more prudent to present things in this fashion, I didn't want to offend her, nor above all to put her in an awkward position with regard to Darren. I'd already done enough damage of that sort.

"Why make this recommendation?" She pursued.

"I suppose I'm not best placed to talk about it."

"If you knew our laws, you would know that it's forbidden to do what he did to you."

"I know. I still don't know all of your laws, but this one, I do know. Nevertheless... What's done is done, and there's no going back. You have to accept it, whether it pleases you or not."

I didn't want to be so harsh, but I didn't see any other way to put an end to this conversation. Put on the spot, Marie was open-mouthed, she hadn't expected such a reaction from me. Alas! The calm was short-lived. Her eyes suddenly changed colour. She was enraged and, I must admit, I didn't exactly want to see an angry vampire. From that moment on, I got up and retreated several steps back.

But she was already up. Her look had become bestial. She bounded towards me like an animal to its prey. Her face was a few centimetres away from mine. My God! Her eyes were as black as night, bloodshot.

"How dare you speak to me in that way?"

I caught sight of her canines with dread. I was paralysed with terror. She shoved into me.

"How did you convince him to transform you? I'm asking you the question for the last time. Answer me!"

I didn't know what to do. I didn't want either to disobey Darren or to anger her further. I tried to think about it... It was a waste of time. She grabbed me by my shoulders, I felt her nails penetrate my flesh.

"You're hurting me!"

"It'll be worse if you don't answer."

"I can't, I'm sorry."

"Let go of her, Marie!" Vic intervened from his counter.

Much like a cat, she went and stood in front of him and let out a howl similar to that which the big cats use to distress their prey. I was petrified, but Vic didn't flinch. The very next second, Darren put himself between her and me. Finally!

"I forbid you to touch her, Marie. Have you understood me?"

"Why is that?"

"She's a part of the family."

"Really? Since when? And since when we do transform humans without even warning the Clan? Since when? Come on, answer me!"

She was hysterical; more so than Darren had imagined. She turned towards the others and shouted:

"Does anybody know about this new law?"

A unanimous 'no' filled the room. All eyes were now turned on us, and more particularly on Darren. Pierre discreetly left the club. Vic closed the door and the curtains. We were locked in. All together. The hour of the council had struck. It was hardly taking place how Darren had anticipated, but we couldn't do anything about it. He turned to me.

"Excuse me, excuse them... Did she hurt you?"

He seemed really saddened by the attitude of his sister. Fortunately, it had been more frightening than painful. I discreetly rubbed my bruised shoulders, I tried to smile. Then, Darren went to the centre of the room, where the others were already waiting for him.

"Lilly, come here!" He called over to me.

I silently complied and sat down near him. What was going to happen next?

Marie opened the debate. She had calmed down and had regained a human appearance. She would outline the facts, then Darren would have a right of reply.

"We established laws for our own safety, which allow us to live in harmony with human beings. Nobody has the right to infringe these laws. Yet, one of them has been violated by the most important person among us, which doesn't excuse him."

She pointed at him as if he was a criminal, then carried on:

"A transformation can be accepted in certain cases, and above all - she insisted on this word - after consultation with the Council. This wasn't done! We were presented with a fait accompli. I don't doubt that there are valid grounds for it, but if we all act in this way, the outcome is chaos and the end of our family. That's why I'm asking Darren to explain to the Council the reasons for his actions."

Darren gulped and presented himself before the assembly.

"It's not completely true," Darren began.

"Are you calling me a liar?"

"Let him speak, Marie," intervened Vic calmly.

"I said that it wasn't completely true, because I received Martin's approval regarding this transformation."

"Why only Martin?" Asked a man I didn't know.

"Because this transformation was done specifically on Lilly's request. She came to find me and told me her story…"

"Well this is the first time I've heard such nonsense! What human being would want a transformation, unless they were crazy?" Henry intervened.

"You see, Lilly, I had warned you: They take you for a madwoman," said Darren.

I nodded in agreement. I preferred to keep silent, as long as I wasn't invited to express myself.

"So what is this story which made you defy so many rules, Darren?" Questioned Marie.

"I'll only tell you what's strictly necessary for you to understand my action. If one day, Lilly wants to tell you more, she'll do so."

"Too easy!" Answered Marie.

"No Marie, it's not easy."

Darren began to lose patience. I didn't understand why his sister was persecuting him. My brother would instead have supported me in a similar situation.

"It's about HER story, Marie. Would you like me to tell yours to everybody, here, now?"

She remained pensive for a few moments.

"No, excuse me."

For the first time since our arrival, Marie lowered her eyes in front of her brother.

"Lilly had a quest, and this brought her to us. You all saw her come here, a few weeks ago. It wasn't a coincidence. For her, from her point of view, it was actually a lucky day. No, she isn't crazy! If she had been, I wouldn't have transformed her. I spoke to Martin about it, and only to him, because Lilly's case is very special. Martin gave me the green light. In a way, this transformation saved her life. Her human life."

I felt him to be pensive, looking for the best words. It wasn't so easy to speak about my transformation without revealing my secrets.

"I understand that you don't accept the dispensation accorded to me by Martin, and this has nothing to do with the fact that I'm important. Martin and I thought hard, we weighed up the pros and the cons. We couldn't see any objection to her request. It happened in the chateau, in safety, far away from everything. Trust me, my friends, and accept Lilly among us. Show her something other than that which she's going through this evening, show her that we're civilized, also that we're capable of helping a human being. You all know as well I do, how difficult the first days are, even when we're consenting. Show her who you really are: My family, my friends, all that I have in this world. All that I believe in. She's trusted me... She's trusted us. Blindly. Repay her for this confidence, please!"

On these words, he sat back down near to me. I had the urge to take his hand, to hold it tightly against me, but I didn't dare to move. He'd stood up to them all. For me. I don't know whether any human had done so much for me before.

All eyes were riveted upon me. What were they waiting for, now? I took my courage in both hands:

"Thanks..."

It was the only word which crossed my lips, and nobody reacted. I followed on:

"It's not just a casual word in the air. I thank you from the bottom of my heart. I'm not asking you to love me, no; only to accept me into your family. You, Darren, you know exactly what your act means to me. I'll be eternally grateful to you for it. I'd like to add that I don't know you all; neither do I know the reasons why Darren's so elevated in your hierarchy, but he deserves it. He's never betrayed you and will not do so. Finally, my last word goes out to Vic, without whom I wouldn't be here this evening. He saved my life twice and he's my friend. A real friend, come what may."

On these words, Vic came over to me, a glass in his hand. He offered it to me and said:

"Welcome, Lilly! Whatever your story may be, if in Darren's estimation it needed to be done, and if you agreed, then that's good enough for me."

"Thanks, Vic."

I took big gulps from the glass which he offered me. It was alcoholic and I risked becoming drunk. Yet, no such thing occurred; alcohol had no effect on vampires! Several people then came over to welcome me officially into the family. Marie debated anew with Darren. Something was apparently still bothering her. Was she jealous or was there another reason? She was his blood sister, but maybe they had something else in common? I didn't know if vampires had a love life, whether they could fall in love. Many questions came to me and, some day or other, it would be necessary to find answers to them.

Little by little, the club emptied, the evening had brought a wealth of emotions for everybody. I let them discuss it all, and settled myself back in the bar where Vic was now taking care of the washing up.

"Tough evening," he said.

"Yes, indeed. Darren had told me that a Council would take place, I hadn't imagined that it would be held so quickly."

"Martin should've been present; that would have calmed things down. For the moment, she hasn't dropped the matter."

"Why does she have to be that way?"

"He's her blood brother. He transformed her, she must feel a betrayal. Since Amélie, nobody else has been transformed. After Amélie, we established laws. It became too dangerous, it seemed that everyone did as they liked. You're the first one for twenty-six years. Marie was bound to be shocked, of course! When you entered this evening, I felt so too at first, but you were with Darren. I told myself that he must have a good reason for it."

He finished his sentence on a smile. Vic was my friend, I could talk about everything and nothing with him. He accepted me as I was and I appreciated him for it. No complications, no arguments, just a sincere friendship, even if we'd only recently got to know each other.

"Are vampires capable of loving? I mean to say… Like humans are?"

"Of course! We're derived from human beings, but our needs and feelings remain the same. At least, me, I don't feel any differently."

"You have a girlfriend?"

"Yes, and she's human besides," he added as naturally as anything. "I love humans, I'd never do them any harm. Some sense a difference, but seem to appreciate it. My girlfriend adores me. I'll introduce her to you, she's very nice."

"I don't doubt it. She doesn't ever ask questions?"

"About what?"

He stood motionless in front of me, his cloth in hand.

"The matter of not eating, for example."

"I make sure that we don't see each other at mealtimes…"

"Yes, of course. And love, it is the same?"

"Physically, you mean?"

"Yes," I said, looking down, a little embarrassed by the way the conversation was going.

He smiled to me again.

"We just have to control certain impulses, otherwise yes, it's just the same."

"What kinds of impulses?"

He gave me a cheeky wink.

"Like to bite, for example."

"I see."

He resumed his washing up and continued:

"Or to restrain our urge to transform into a vampire, following the surge of adrenalin. These sorts of little details."

"Like Marie did this evening?"

"Exactly. You learn quickly!"

"I had no choice. I was terrified, you know!"

"I know. I tried to help you, but she's tough."

"Do we become powerful due to the one who transformed us?"

"Partially, yes. After that, it's by exploiting our gifts."

"Our gifts…?"

"Yes, some of us possess gifts; others don't. That's just how it is. Marie is very strong."

"And me?"

"You've inherited Darren's gifts. Now, it's up to you to perceive yours, those which are your own. Time will help you to discover them."

He carefully wiped his glasses and then arranged them on the shelves. I followed each of his actions, while continuing to harass him with questions.

"And what are they, Darren's gifts?"

"It's for him to tell you, Lilly."

"Oh, okay. I didn't want to be indiscreet."

"I know, don't worry!"

Vic smiled ceaselessly. A little bit like Darren. I didn't know the circumstances of their transformation, but in that era, they certainly wouldn't have had the choice. Nevertheless, they seemed happy to be vampires. After all, this life was well worth another one!

The ride back was silent. I took advantage of it to observe the night as I'd never seen it before. My vision was different, even better than in broad daylight! The car was going at a brisk pace. Nevertheless, if my eyes alighted on a tree or a window, everything seemed to be in slow motion and I had plenty of time to observe what was happening. It was a strange and superb sensation. A positive point in my physical state, because until a few days ago, I wore glasses. Since then, I've been able to see at night, what more could I ask?

Darren was concentrating on the road and on his thoughts. The evening had been tough for everyone. I didn't dare to break the silence, so I continued to look at the scenery. Nevertheless, without thinking about it, I said suddenly:

"I don't feel the need to sleep..."

"It's normal. In fact, we don't sleep, rather we go into a form of slumber. Our senses, they stay on alert."

I felt him suddenly to be somewhere else. It worried me.

"Are you all right?"

"Yes. I'm reflecting on things, that's all."

I returned his smile. I didn't want to disturb him. What's more, we'd almost arrived and it wasn't necessary to engage in a conversation now.

Passing in front of Hector's house, I saw that everything was switched off. Night constitutes a time of slumber for all. Even if we don't sleep, I suppose our bodies still need to rest.

I went back to my bedroom. I liked this chateau, I felt safe here. In the wardrobe, I found other clothes which belonged to me. My apartment had doubtless been visited, because I had no memory of having brought so much for a simple weekend. So I slipped on a tracksuit as well as a sweatshirt and decided to go back into Darren's library. This place was magical, and I hadn't yet had the time to look at everything.

Arriving at the door, I didn't consider it necessary to knock, persuading myself that nobody would answer.

"Could I have forgotten to wish you good night, Lilly?"

"Oh! Pardon me. I believed that you were in your room. I'll come back again later."

I was going to leave the room, but he kept me there.

"No, come in!"

He sat at a desk which I hadn't spotted this morning. I took a seat facing him. As usual, he looked at me, smiling, and waited for me to speak. After all, I had intruded into his universe.

I returned his smile without saying a word. I simply looked around me. To tell the truth, he intimidated me. Did he realise it? He dived back into his papers. The administration for such a residence must be considerable: To make sure that nothing gets missed, that everything is paid. And all this, for years… Perhaps longer!

"How old are you, Darren?"

He raised his nose from his papers with a look of surprise.

"I was born in Dublin on the 18th of April, 1845, of Matthew and Elise Owen. So I'm 167 years old."

"You don't look it. When were you transformed?"

Darren understood that he would have no peace if he wasn't going answer my questions. He closed the register, put it in front of him and crossed his arms on his desk.

"I was transformed in 1876, I was thirty-one years old."

"How did it happen?"

"I'd spent the evening in a pub in Dublin. I went quietly back home, a little bit tipsy, when my path crossed that of Martin's."

"The doctor?"

"Yes, he'd come out from a seminar and had doubtless nothing better to do than to enlarge his family. He chose me that night."

"He chose you and you accepted?"

"You know, I hadn't any choice. He set upon me, I had no chance. He would have been able to kill me, but he transformed me. Don't ask me why, I don't even know myself and I've never asked him the question. Then, he brought me back to France, in his luggage."

"And your parents, your family?"

"My parents died when I was still a baby, following the great famine which affected Ireland, in the year of my birth. My sister and I were taken in by my aunt, but she didn't have the means to feed us. So I ended up in Dublin, in a foundation. That was a good thing, in the end, because my aunt probably wouldn't have been able to offer me the education which I received there."

He gazed out through the window. He was mulling over his Irish years.

"Do you bear any grudge against Martin?"

"No, the only difficult thing for me, was knowing that my sister was in Ireland, while I was in France. She was my only family and I missed her enormously. That's the reason why I went back there, to look for her two years later."

"Marie?"

"Yes, Marie is my sister in every sense of the word."

"You gave her the choice?"

He looked at me sadly. I was reminding him of painful memories. It was maybe too much, after the events of this evening.

"She didn't want to follow me. I didn't want to lose her again. She was everything to me."

"It was selfish, as a reaction!"

I immediately regretted these words…

"Please excuse me… I didn't want to…"

"No it's okay. I felt very guilty for many years. Now, I no longer regret it. She would've died if I hadn't done it."

"Yes, but that's the way of things."

"Would you not be eager, you, to transform a loved one, to bring them eternal life so that you'd be together?"

"I don't know, I'm sorry. Ask me this question in a few years' time. And Marie, how did she find it?"

"At the beginning, it was hard for her. Especially because of the language, when she found herself in Paris with me. But regarding her condition as in being a vampire, she's never regretted it. Much to my surprise, actually."

"How old was she?"

"Thirty-three. We're twins."

This explained many things. Twins have links which other brothers and sisters don't have.

"For twins, you don't resemble each other."

"That's lucky! We're not the same gender," he added, laughing. "Furthermore, Marie dyes her hair. Don't tell her that I spoke to you about it…"

"No, no."

His attitude amused me. He worshipped his sister. It's probably the reason why he needed her approval so much.

"Her attitude this evening saddens you?"

"No, it was justified. Also, she doesn't know the ins and outs of it all. Now, she's reassured, even if she remains a little bit jealous. She doesn't like seeing me in the company of a woman… She's exclusive. You'll like her. She's adorable, but a little bit hot-blooded, if I may say so."

"What would've happened if she had bitten me?"

"Nothing. You would've had some pain at the time, that's all."

"And you, did you suffer when I bit you?"

"No, Lilly. For the last time: NO."

"All right, let's not speak about it anymore."

"Thank you."

He reopened his register and scrawled some notes on the side. I was surprised that he didn't use a computer, but after all, I didn't even know what he was doing exactly. I found a well-chosen moment to wish him a good night, and went back to my room to rest.

The night was peaceful, a great silence reigned over the chateau. It was extremely relaxing. I adored this place.

6

A vampire doesn't sleep, certainly, but the slumber is so deep, that I had no memory of the hours I'd spent in my bed. I'd rested though, that's what was important.

I took a quick shower, pulled on my jeans and headed for the kitchen... At least, I hoped I'd find it!

Hector was busying himself around the stoves. I didn't understand what he was doing there, because we don't eat. I didn't ask him the question, I'd find out in the end.

"Hello, Hector."

"Hello, Miss Lilly."

"You can call me Lilly, you know."

"I like addressing you that way," he said with a big smile.

I didn't insist.

"May I have a glass of milk, please?"

My sentence was barely finished; the glass was already in front of me, accompanied by two white capsules."

"Do you have the gift of reading thoughts?"

"If the person is near me, it comes to me."

"It's useful. Might I ask you a question?"

"Of course."

"What are they, these capsules? Yesterday at the Club, Vic also brought me two. Which I didn't take, by the way."

"These capsules contain blood. Hasn't Darren spoken to you about it yet?"

I remained pensive.

"Blood, you say?"

At that moment, Darren made his entrance into the kitchen and greeted us with a simple wave. It seemed to me that the night had been short for him. How long had he stayed in the library to mull over his memories and his papers?

"Freeze-dried, Lilly. You have to take at least two a day to keep on good form."

"I understand, now... "No liquid blood!" Where does it come from, this blood?"

"From the blood bank. It's the surest way to get healthy blood. You can swallow them with complete peace of mind."

"I didn't take any yesterday, but I didn't feel unwell for it!"

"Your daily portion was in the milk which we took in front of the fireplace."

"The taste was no different from that of pure milk..."

"No, this blood has no taste, no colour. It avoids temptation, you understand?"

"Yes, I believe so."

It ensured that ill-intentioned vampires didn't become tempted. I supposed that the smell of blood must continue to fuel certain appetites. It was a smart solution.

"Did you sleep well, Darren?"

"It was short, but restorative."

"I have to go to my apartment in Paris. Do you believe that's possible today?"

"Yes. Besides, I have business to be settled there, that fits in well."

"Great! I'm going to get ready."

Five minutes later, I was in the hall waiting for him.

"Ha ha, you seem to me to be in a great hurry, this morning!" He called out as he rushed down the stairs.

"To be honest, I was ready. I just had to get my keys."

"Okay, let's go!"

Again, passing the gate in the car, I tried to spot Amélie thereabouts, but without success. For the moment, this woman remained a mystery.

"Why do you need to go to your apartment?" He asked, while we were pulling onto the road.

"I'd like to fetch my laptop PC and if possible, my car."

I hesitated on the last point, his response proved me right.

"For your computer or anything else, that's okay; but as for the car, it's premature. It's not a lack of trust, but I need to keep an eye on you constantly. You still don't know your reactions in the face of stress or in other situations. I prefer to keep you near me for the moment."

"I thought so. How long will that be for?"

"You're bored already?"

"Not at all. Only that I don't want to bother you every time I want to go somewhere."

"You don't bother me. Look, I'm going to leave you at your apartment; as soon as you've finished, call me and I'll come and look for you. It's simple and it's no problem for me."

"It's a deal!"

The rest of the journey passed silently. A strange feeling came over me on seeing my building. I had the feeling that it wasn't the same place any more. I no longer saw it in the same way, it was really strange. Darren must have sensed my confusion.

"Would you like me to come with you, Lilly?"

"No, it'll pass, thank you."

I took his hand, planted a kiss on it and left the car. I astonished myself at such a gesture of affection. I felt a little embarrassed. He seemed surprised, but delighted.

Turning the key in the lock, the strange impression persisted, but as soon as I closed the door, everything faded away.

The problem was only to be found outside; in here, I was safe. I phoned Darren immediately to share my feeling with him. He admitted to me that he too had felt something different compared to his first visit. I was still unable to define this difference, it was new. He asked me to hurry and to call him back as soon as I was ready.

I made a quick tour of the apartment, I gathered up my things and tended to my plants. Then, I opened my mail. Nothing very important, apart from my appointment with the doctor. He always sent me a little reminder. He expected me on November 30th at four o'clock. As he would be going on holiday in December, he had moved the appointment forwards.

I looked around; everything was in order, I could call Darren back.

Ten minutes later, he rang the doorbell. No need to look in the peephole, I'd sensed him, it was very handy! He entered my apartment just as he'd done a few weeks earlier and took hold of the bag which I'd put on the floor. I took my laptop and closed the door.

We left with this shared impression: Something or somebody, here, was different. I then told Darren about my new appointment with the doctor. He took note.

"I still have something to do. Shall I drop you at the club?"

"Oh! Yes, a small coffee will do me good."

Vic was loyally at his post behind his counter. There were a few customers, humans and vampires. I liked this ability to differentiate people. I sat down in my usual place, even if it reminded me of the painful events of the day before. I felt good there, I had complete vision around the room.

"Hello Lilly, what can I get for you?"

"A coffee with milk, please."

"Consider it done!" He said, skillfully making a cup spin around.

I took my laptop out of its case to do some searches on the internet. I wanted to discover how and where Darren had grown up. I'd noticed the Wi-Fi hotspot over the bar on the first day. I connected there without difficulty, then I typed in his date of birth, followed by the word Dublin.

I had a very wide choice, but my eyes were drawn to one title: "Nearly a million deaths, following the great famine which raged in Ireland!" Darren's family had been a part of it. The article also mentioned a large number of emigrants. They'd had two alternatives: Death or flight. Those who had stayed knew only suffering. Hardly surprising that the Irish people had risen up against the British regime! It would be interesting to ask Darren to what extent he'd participated in this uprising. Maybe I would ask him one day.

I continued for a long time reading and contemplating images of that era. His transformation had taken place in the

Victorian period. I remained full of admiration for the dresses of those years, the luxurious balls reserved for the very rich. But suddenly, I sensed him entering the club. He sat down by my side, silently.

"You're curious, Lilly."

"Fortunately, otherwise I would never have found you!"

"That's true. One point to you."

"I wanted to look at the era of your birth and that of your transformation. You don't hold it against me?"

"Not at all. I have the internet in the chateau also, you know."

"Really? Why do you do your accounts on a written register, then?"

"Those accounts are special. I don't want to leave other trails on that register."

"Darren, I'd like... How shall I say?"

"Try. You always succeed with it very well," he said, smiling as usual.

"Well... If you'll allow me, I'd like to organize a party. It would help the others to get to know me. What do you think about it?"

"A party? What kind of party?"

"I don't know..."

"Yes. You know very well. Come on, tell me what you really think. I'd like to hear you."

I fixed him right in the eyes.

"Don't read my thoughts!"

"I'm not doing that, I promise."

"I don't believe you."

He looked at me without turning a hair, waiting for my response.

"A ball."

His silence put me ill-at-ease. I clarified it:

"Costumed!"

"All right."

"That's it?"

"Yes, I agree. It's been a long time since a reception was hosted at the chateau. I'll let you take care of organising it; I'll take care of sending out the invitations as soon as you've given me the text. See Hector regarding the decor, or whatever else you'll need. It's a very good idea, Lilly!"

"Really? I'm happy you agree with it."

He was still smiling at me. Honestly, he seemed content. I was in seventh heaven.

The journey back to the chateau was rather silent. I would suddenly have to think about so many things. I was still stunned with surprise, his agreement had encouraged me. I wished very much to have this grand ball! But first I had to draft the invitations. Fortunately, I had my laptop. But in passing the gate, I realised that I didn't even know the name of this property...

"Tell me...? Does your chateau have a name?"

"It's the Nerfel chateau, built in the middle of the sixteenth century and renovated under my care around 1950. I regularly carry out works to maintain it in good condition and especially bring it some of the modernisation which we need. The bathrooms, for example. But certain rooms have stayed like they were when I arrived here. I just renovated them while keeping the spirit of the period."

"Do you like the architecture and decor?"

Every question, and every answer taught me more about him.

"Yes, but I especially like to keep the spirit of the place I first saw. I chose it because I liked it. So, I keep it that way if I can."

"From what I've seen, you do that very well."

This time, it was me who smiled at him. Unusually, he parked in front of the castle. Did he have to go back out again?

"Come," he said, "I'm going to show you your ballroom."

He seemed as motivated as I was with this idea of a party. We went across to the other side of the chateau. I knew very few rooms, after all. I felt that he was very proud of this place. We were getting to know each other in the course of events and I admit that this way of going about it had a certain charm.

He stopped suddenly in front of an immense double door.

"Close your eyes."

I obeyed without saying a word.

"Are you ready?"

"Yes."

I heard him open the first half of the double doors, followed by the other half. A cool breeze came over me. He took me by the hand and slowly pulled me in. The number of steps to reach what I thought to be the centre of the room was considerable. He stood still.

"Can I open my eyes, now? I'm so impatient."

"Yes, you can."

"My God!"

The room was gigantic. I counted at least twenty windows. The ceiling, too, was excessively high. I asked myself why the rooms were so high in this era. The walls were faced in a light wood, the colour of honey, and varnished, right up to the middle. The space was ornamented with paintings up to a second level of panelling, and then finally came the ceiling. It was magnificent. Big double curtains, black in colour, hung at every window. The place was magical. The room was empty, except for a grand piano. It looked like a toy in such a big space.

"Now that you know the room, think about everything which you have to plan. You have carte blanche. Hector is there to assist you."

"An orchestra?"

I felt like a child who just received the most beautiful of presents.

"If you wish… It's your ball, organise it as you please. But don't take a long time with the invitations! Even vampires want to be impeccable. And since your ball will be costumed…"

"Can I choose the Victorian era?"

"I slightly suspected that."

"This doesn't bother you? If it brings you bad memories, I can change it…"

"No, it's perfect, I already have my suit. So I won't have to run all over Paris trying to be perfect."

"You kept your old clothes?"

"Yes, I keep everything in the attic. A real little treasure. I even rent them out for the film industry. It's very useful. I'm recognised as having one of the most complete collections."

"I didn't know."

"It's true, you don't know much about me; like me, I don't know much about you. But we have all of time to get to know each other."

He ended his sentence looking me right in the eyes. His look made me lower mine. I blushed a little maybe. At least, I had that impression.

"Do you also possess feminine clothes?"

"The most beautiful in the whole place. Come and see!"

We took a good ten minutes to get to the attic, this chateau was so large, and its steps, so high. A few days earlier, this spiral staircase would have exhausted me. It ended with a heavy wooden and wrought iron door.

The room which we discovered was just like the rest of the chateau: Immense and totally white. It was air-conditioned. The installation must have been expensive, but it was necessary to preserve all these clothes in the best condition.

"They're classified by period: To the right for women, to the left for men. I don't suppose it concerns you, but in the dressing room, to the right at the far end of the room, you'll also find clothes for children classified by age and by sex. Follow me!"

He took me by my hand and led me towards a long, illuminated display cabinet.

"You'll find all the jewels and other accessories here which any woman could dream of."

"I'm still standing here open-mouthed."

"Yes, I see. Don't you like it?"

"Of course I do!"

I turned to him, we were now face to face. Barely a few centimetres separated our faces.

"Darren, you know my musical tastes, right?"

"Yes, at least, partially..."

Apparently he hadn't understood my remark.

"Don't you see that all this corresponds exactly to something that I've always liked? Look at these jewels: A great deal of them are of the Gothic style, the most beautiful I've ever seen."

I went over to the dresses.

"Look at this blue velvet, at these laces, at this finish... In what way could it ever displease me? And this corset? What a marvel! If I could do so, I'd dress like that every day. It completely corresponds to me. I have the feeling of being in my own universe!"

He looked at me fixedly, with a bizarre smile.

"You take me for a madwoman, right?"

"Not at all!"

"Is anything wrong?"

He was suddenly different. I would have bet that his eyes had changed colour.

"No, I'm happy that all this pleases you. To be honest, it's beyond my expectations."

"What's the matter then? I sense a problem..."

"No, all's perfect."

He lied, for sure. I tried to give him back his confidence.

"What costume are you going to wear?"

"I shall choose it according to your dress."

"So you'll be my dance partner?"

"Naturally! You can try all the dresses you wish. You can even wear them all the time."

"Thank you! You've fulfilled one of my oldest dreams... I've more than one friend who'd be wild with jealousy."

"I do believe it. I have to leave you, now. Will you be able to find your way back?"

"I hope so. Thanks Darren."

"You're welcome."

He left the room silently. What detail had disturbed him so? A memory? Had a piece of jewellery reminded him of some event?

My choice came to a black-bluish, velvet dress. I put it on as well as I could... So many laces, and buttons... I succeeded despite all of these and decided to return to the ballroom. I was still barefooted, because I hadn't found any shoes. What's more he hadn't spoken about any. If my memory served me correctly, it was right at the end of the staircase.

Yes I'd remembered well. I pushed the door open again and crossed the room with my eyes closed. I tried to imagine myself at the ball, in the arms of Darren, and I realised suddenly that it might have been me that had disturbed him.

I settled down at the piano. From there, I spotted my own reflection in a window. This dress was magnificent! I decided to put some of my hair up into a bun, then I began to play. Notes resounded around the room, I let my fingers run along the keyboard. I'd never played so well; with so much ease, agility. Such was my concentration that I didn't hear him come in, but I felt him the moment he sat down near me.

At that instant, a strange sensation came over me. I saw my nails metamorphosing. He put a hand on mine. Immediately, the room was filled with a heavy silence.

"You have to learn to control your feelings, Lilly. Some of them can change you physically. That's all very well when you're here in the chateau, there's no danger, but outside..."

"Yes, Vic had a word with me. Alas, I've no idea how to channel off these external signs. I don't even know which feelings can change my physical appearance, nor to what extent."

"Anger and attraction are the most difficult feelings to hide for a young vampire. You'll recall... Marie, the other evening... It's the kind of physical transformation that occurs if we don't pay attention and if we don't control ourselves... That's what just happened to you. Music affects you greatly, in particular the piano. I remember it myself, at the club, when I played for you. Even beneath your human form, it was noticeable."

"What can I do? I don't want others to be able to guess my feelings. It's intimate, you understand?"

"I understand perfectly. The wisest thing, is to avoid risky situations in public. If you feel yourself becoming angry, go away from the source of it."

"That's what you did in the attic, is that right?"

"I wasn't angry."

"No, of course. In this case, how do you channel away the transformations?"

"Hey! Well, apart from fleeing, there's concentration. You continue doing what you started, but you concentrate on something other than the source of the emotion itself. For example, if music is the source, you concentrate on an object. The curtains, for example. Try it!"

I began playing again, this time concentrating on the curtains. However as the source of my turmoil wasn't the music, I had to concentrate on several things at once without giving anything away. That's when Darren started to play too. We were playing a duet. I tried to stay focused on the curtains, but the music intoxicated me.

I then felt my vision changing. I made no effort to stop the transformation, because I wasn't anywhere public, just in the safety of the chateau. Again, my nails lengthened, they took on an ochre colour. I had to alter my touch on the keys. I heard the rain striking the windows. Its beating blended with the sound of the piano. I was completely captivated by the moment, incapable of controlling anything, but I felt good...

We played in symbiosis. He wouldn't have wanted to stop this moment either, I sensed it. We carried on like this until the end of the piece, then I rested my hands on my knees. A few seconds were enough for my nails to retract and for my vision to recover.

He was right. Perhaps it was the music...

"Forgive me, I didn't stop it."

"How did you feel this time?"

"I felt good. The music along with the rain... It was intoxicating. It was very pleasant. If I'd controlled myself, would I have felt the same thing?"

"Yes, but without the physical changes."

"All right. In that case, I have to learn to do this."

"Yes, you must. For yourself and for the family. As a security measure."

"I know, Darren."

He got up, stepped back, looking at me from every angle. It became embarrassing.

"Show me your dress…"

I too stood up, but I lifted the underskirts of the dress for fear of damaging them. He watched me in admiration and walked around me to get a better look.

"You're perfect… Very pretty. It's absolutely your style. But why are you barefooted?"

"I didn't find any shoes."

He roared with laughter, I felt stupid.

"Stop laughing at me!"

"Forgive me. Tell me, do you know how to waltz?"

"Of course not! What an idea! Are you going to carry on laughing for long, or are you going to show me how?"

"I'm going to show you!"

He came over to me, he seemed happy to have made me angry. Then he put my left hand on his shoulder and grabbed my right hand. I felt his right hand on my hip.

"I'm going to teach you a three-step waltz. This dance is made up of three steps. The first one is the longest, both of the following ones are quieter, but each step has the same duration. It's simple, follow me."

"Okay."

He stamped on the floor to oblige me to look at him. The banging resounded in the empty room.

"You mustn't watch your feet. Look at me!"

"I'll try, but I've never waltzed, me!"

"Everything has to start somewhere. Ready?"

I nodded in agreement.

"One, two, three... One, two, three... One, two, three... It's good... You're doing well for a twenty-first century woman!"

"Thanks!"

I was hooked, we were dancing without music in an immense empty ballroom. He must miss his own era... We still hadn't really spoken about it, and I could be mistaken. I'd need quite a lot of time to get to know him, his life was so long! He fascinated me, I'm afraid. What would happen when I would be back at work, far from him and the others? Were they all going to forget me?

There were lots of things which I hadn't thought about before venturing into this story. I should be strong.

7

The weather was very beautiful, this morning. I settled down in the park, on my low wall, with my laptop computer. This time, nothing could happen to me.

It was high time to draft my invitation card, because the ball was getting close. My iPod to my ears, I tried to concentrate on the matter, but this wasn't to be so easy.

"Your breakfast, Miss Lilly."

Hector put a tray down beside me, with my glass of milk and my capsules. How had he known that I was here?

"Thank you, but I was going to come, you know..."

"No, it's very good like this. It changes my routine. How do you find the gardens?"

I was pleased by this question. He was becoming used to me.

"Magnificent! Who takes care of them?"

I felt that a privileged moment was coming. Perhaps I'd get to know a little more about Amélie.

"My wife and myself."

"Just the two of you manage all of this?"

"Yes, Amélie adores gardening. She spends all of her time here."

"Would you introduce her to me one day?"

"Of course, Miss Lilly!"

With these last words, he left me; the conversation was closed. I'd still learnt nothing, but I hadn't given up, that wouldn't have been how I was. Then I concentrated again on my invitation card, I wolfed down my milk and my "meal". I needed it more than I'd anticipated.

* * *

I decided to submit my design for the invitations to Darren. I'd kept it simple, I hoped that would please him too.

I found him in the lounge, the room bestowed with a fireplace. He was on the phone. It was the second time that I'd seen him on the phone. He spoke in English. He signalled to me to sit down. I did so, my laptop on my knees.

"Excuse me," he said, hanging up.

"No problem. I wanted to show you the invitation."

He came up to me and sat down on the armrest of the armchair. I pointed the computer in his direction.

"It's very good, just perfect. You should have stated that you're the one who's doing the inviting."

Invitation
The hosts of the Chateau de Nerfel
Invite you on Saturday, November 21st at 11pm
To a grand Victorian ball
And ask you to honour them with your presence
Period costume required.

"No. This isn't my home, here. I wouldn't want to incur the wrath of your sister."

"I understand, you're prudent... Well, I'm going to print it. Hector can even send them today. You didn't waste any time, so tell me... Have you thought about anything else?"

"Were you planning on inviting any humans?"

"Some people can come, yes."

"In that case, should I plan a buffet?"

"Good thinking. Vic will help you with the choice of dishes and petit fours, he adores doing such things. He loves humans so much that one wonders whether he's not a little bit envious," he said jokingly.

"As soon as the invitations have been sent, I'll have something else to ask him."

He looked at me. I hinted at half a smile.

"No, you're not to know!"

"Okay," he answered with an air of sadness.

"If I tell you everything, where's the surprise?"

"As you wish."

He gave up, fuming, and headed to the printer.

"What should I do with the dress which I wore yesterday?"

"Give it to Amélie, she'll take care of it."

I went over to join him. The printing had been quick and the quality was impeccable. I was proud of my little creation.

"I printed three hundred; that should be enough."

"Three hundred?"

"For a ball, that's a minimum."

"It's going to be extremely expensive...?"

I looked downwards. Not only couldn't I allow myself such an expense, but I hadn't thought about it at all.

"Don't worry about it, okay?"

"Thanks."

He sat down in his armchair, I did likewise.

"You know, Lilly, this situation is different from how I'd imagined."

"How do you mean?"

"Usually, with a human, either we transform them or we kill them, and that's all. With you, it's different: You're here, you're trying to become integrated into the family, you're happy, cheerful... The few people in the family who know you, love you."

"Except maybe Marie."

"Yes, yes, she loves you. It is just a little bit difficult for her. I was surprised to find Hector smiling to himself. Vic adores you. Things are taking an unexpected turn. And over and above it all, you like the life!"

"All thanks to you! Without this transformation, my life would still be only suffering. But you're right: I didn't imagine that things would be so lovely either. I'm living a real fairy tale. I find myself in an environment which suits me perfectly, although it's temporary. So, I take one hundred percent advantage of it."

"Why temporary?"

"I'll have to return to my normal life... In a month's time, I have to go back to work!"

"And...?"

"I'll have to come to terms with my new life with humans, on my own."

"But I... We will always be here for you, Lilly. I'll never be far away, trust me. Your human life will only be a cover. It'll simply allow you, in their eyes, to exist still. But in a few years' time, you'll be free to do what you want, without caring about them. When they'll have died. You can stay in your work for no more than ten years, you understand why?"

"Yes, I'm no longer going to age physically, my appearance is going to stay the same, which could arouse suspicions."

"Exactly…"

Hector appeared at the door.

"He is here, Sir."

"One moment, Hector. Lilly, I have an appointment. Go and find Amélie for the dress. We'll see each other later to speak about the ball or about what you'll want."

"Very well."

I headed towards the door, it would be a good opportunity to meet Amélie.

"No; go this way instead," he said, pointing at a French window which led out to the park.

"Why?"

"Please…"

I obeyed and went out by the route which he'd shown me. After a few metres, voices resounded inside my head. I stopped and tried to work out where they were coming from. Darren's visitor had just entered the lounge.

"Hello Darren," he said.

"Hello Alexandre. To what do I owe the honour of your visit?"

"I heard that you had a new protégée."

"News travels fast."

"It's rather surprising considering your family: you love human beings so much that you do them no harm. Why such a change?"

"It's a long story, which isn't your concern, Alexandre. Don't tell me that you came all this way just for this? One moment, Alexandre…"

Darren came out, stared at me and approached me slowly, turning around to be sure of not being followed.

"Lilly, it isn't nice to eavesdrop!"

"I didn't know… These voices in my head gave me such a surprise, that I stopped where I was. I didn't mean to be indiscreet, forgive me. I got this gift from you?"

"Probably, go and see Amélie, now."

"All right."

I left rapidly. I skirted around the house to get the dress from my bedroom and went steadily towards Hector's house, without looking back. I was a little frightened by the hostility of Darren's visitor. He wasn't part of the family, this was for certain.

I knocked gently at the door of the little gatehouse. A very young woman came to open the door. She was very beautiful and had long, totally blonde hair. Her face was very sweet, but her gaze was very strange.

"Hello, I'm looking for Amélie."

"Hello Lilly, that's me. I've been expecting you. Darren told me that you'd come. Is this the dress which I have to take care of?"

"Yes, please."

She took it in her hands and touched it in a manner which surprised me.

"It's very beautiful. Do you wish to wear it during the ball?"

"I don't know yet, there are still so many in the attic to choose from. Will you be coming to it?"

"Of course, I wouldn't miss it for the world."

"Very good. In that case, there'll be at least four of us," I said, smiling.

"No, you'd be surprised. They'll all come."

"Really?"

"Vampires have a bad failing: They're very curious," she stated, whispering.

"I still have a lot to learn, you know."

"All in good time. Hector will bring you the dress tomorrow," she concluded.

"Thank you, Amélie."

"You're welcome."

"Why don't you ever come to the chateau?"

"You see; vampires, even young ones, are curious. Don't worry, we'll have plenty of time to get to know each other."

"All right, please excuse me."

"May I give you some advice? Stop excusing yourself all the time. Never show your weaknesses to another vampire, even if this one does have an angelic face."

"Okay, I'll take your advice!"

This woman was more than strange. She made me feel uneasy, something about her wasn't normal. I had shivers down my spine all the way back to the chateau. What's more, unless I was obliged to do so, I wouldn't be returning to that house anytime soon.

Darren's visitor, this Alexandre, had left. This was a very good thing. He seemed no more determined than Amélie to accept me into the vampire family. I tried to chase all these thoughts out of my head and so concentrate again on the ball. A shadow hung over me nevertheless and I was unable to get rid of this bad premonition. I left to take refuge in my room and stayed there to lie down for several hours.

"Knock knock, can I come in?" Asked Darren.

"Of course," I said, sitting myself up in bed.

Darren poked his head around the open chink of the door.

"Will you accompany me to the club?"

"Yes, I need to breathe a little fresh air."

"What happened with Amélie? Did she do something wrong? You can tell me everything."

He sat down on the edge of my bed. I brought my knees up towards me, enveloped them with my arms and rested my head on the top.

"No, she was perfect."

"You're lying, Lilly. Amélie is far from being perfect. What happened such that you came to take refuge here?"

"Nothing, I swear to you. The dress will be ready tomorrow."

"It that everything?"

"Yes."

He got up, infuriated.

"Why don't I believe you?"

"I don't know."

He leant over towards me, arms on each side of my knees. He looked me straight in the eyes.

"What did she do or say? Answer me."

"Nothing, I promise you. It was her gaze which frightened me, that's all. And also, this conversation with your friend Alexandre."

"He's not my friend, just an acquaintance. Lilly, I'm going to tell you something about Amélie."

He sat back down on the edge of the bed. I would now know at last, but not from the mouth of the person who was supposed to be informing me.

"When Hector transformed Amélie, there was a complication. He hadn't ever attempted this without our help, but he considered himself stronger than the others. He transformed her here, in my absence. When the second phase began, Amélie was alone in the kitchen. You noticed how strong your cramps were? As there was nobody to keep hold of her as I did for you, she accidentally burned her face. Above all, her eyes. We have the power to regenerate, but not when subjected to fire. It's the worst thing for us. The injuries were too severe. When I returned that evening, it was too late. I did all that I could so that she regained the face which you know now, but she's blind for all eternity."

"That's horrible! How didn't I notice her blindness?"

"Amélie now possesses the gift of clairvoyance, a gift, moreover, which she continues to develop over the course of time. If you don't know what happened, you can't guess that she's blind."

"I understand better now, this strange look that she gave me. And her attitude as well. She's… How shall I say?... A little bit cold."

"She'll get used to you. Time heals all wounds. Show no compassion for her; at least not in her presence."

"I know, she's already given me that advice. She told me never to show my weaknesses, especially in front of a vampire with an angelic air."

"Why this advice?"

"I apologised, I no longer know what for."

"She's not wrong. Up you get, come on, let's go to play and listen to a little music. That soothes the savage beast, it seems. Do you want to drive?"

"Oh yes!"

I jumped off the bed. He threw me the keys to his sports car. What an odd feeling to sit down behind the wheel of a sports coupe! I was delighted. He'd chosen the music to please me, that was certain: "Within Temptation". I turned to him smiling; he was smiling at me without restraint.

"Do you want the sat-nav?"

"No, you're my guide."

"Get a move on then, or we're going to be late."

"Don't tempt me, please."

I took the car along the route leading to Hector's house. This time, I passed the gate without a glance. I knew that I had nothing to see there. As soon as I passed the gate, I put my foot down and a feeling of freedom came over me. An hour and a half later, I parked the car in the place reserved for Darren, in front of the club door.

"Perfect driving! However, I'll be sending you the photos from the speed cameras, if I receive them."

"I didn't break any speed limits!"

"Of course, Fangio!"

"Who?"

"Forget it, you weren't even born."

Always a gentleman, he waited for me to go first into the club.

"Whatever you do, don't change yourself, Lilly."

He had the same look as in the attic.

"As long nothing or no-one obliges me otherwise, I'll try to stay myself."

"Perfect. Let's go."

The club was full, we were late. Darren headed straight for the stage where the rest of the group was waiting for him. Vic smiled at me and showed me a free table on the left side of the room. He brought me a glass of milk and sat down beside me.

"How's it going, Lilly?"

"Very well, and you?"

"Perfect, business is good at the moment. Nothing more to say."

"I'm happy here. Honestly. These works have maybe done some good?"

"Who knows? Now then, this ball? Wonderful idea you had there. What can I do to help you?"

"You already know? Yes, how stupid of me! The invitation, right?"

"No, I haven't received it yet. On the contrary, Darren called to tell me that my help would be precious to you."

"He's not wrong. I'd like you to take care of the catering."

I whispered to him:

"There will be humans, you see?"

"I know. How many human dinner guests?"

"No idea."

I was about to apologise, but I decided otherwise, following Amélie's advice.

"It doesn't matter. Next...?"

"I'd like some music. A group or a good DJ. Do you know any?"

"We could start with a group. Then a DJ. But as it's a ball, you should adapt the music to your Victorian theme a little. I'd say that the opening of the ball should be done to..."

"A waltz!"

"For example, yes. By the way, do you know how to waltz?"

"Of course! With a bit more practice, I'll be fine out there."

"Okay. So; we'll open the ball with a few waltzes, then a musical group and/or a DJ. That seems to be what you want?"

"Perfect. Don't speak of this to Darren, I want to surprise him."

"Cross my heart and hope to die!" He said, going through the motions as he spoke.

"All right, I believe you."

"Lilly, I can ask you an indiscreet question?"

"You're my friend, I can't refuse you anything."

I really did think this. We'd hit it off with one another.

"What's your relationship with Darren?"

"There's no relationship. I'd say that he educates me and I like that. I owe him a lot and I don't want to disappoint him. We're getting to know each other. It's very funny, sometimes."

"What do you feel for him, then?"

"Admiration, respect. I'd like to give him the equivalent of what he's given me, but I'll never be able to do that. So, I try in my own way to please him. Why do you ask? Did I do something wrong?"

"No, not at all. Martin engendered us at about the same time, so in a way we're brothers. Darren takes care of me and I take care of him. I know him very well and I can see that recently, something or somebody has changed him... And I think that it's you."

"Does it bother you?"

"Not at all, on the contrary. I just wanted to make sure everything was all right. For example, it's the first time I've seen someone else driving his car. It's exceptional, the confidence he has in you! Even me, he's never let me borrow it."

"Really, I'm flattered. You know, yesterday, he showed me his collection of clothes. I sensed something different about him, but he didn't want to tell me what had happened. He assured me that all was well, but I'm sure he lied."

"Wait, I'll come back; there are lots of people at the bar."

"Okay."

I took this opportunity to watch Darren playing. He was staring at me, his expression was strange. It was as if he were lost in another world. I neither wanted, nor was I particularly able, to tell Vic of the confusion I'd felt the day before, playing the piano near to him; my transformation in his presence. It was an intimate moment between him and me.

"*Are you sorting things out with Vic there?*" he said from afar.

"*Yes, I believe that we've gone through more or less all that we had to plan for. Tell me, how do you do this?*"

"*In the same way as you do. Don't speak about this gift, keep it for your own advantage. Would you like us to play any song in particular?*"

"*I don't like enough Jazz to know a piece that way, as you well know. Whereas, to suddenly play some Rock would risk displeasing somebody, I'm afraid.*"

"*Yes, you're right.*"

"How do you manage to speak to me, play, and give the rest of the world the impression that you're still with them?"

"Concentration. Remember what I told you."

"Yes."

I smiled to him and I sensed that he smiled too. Vic was right, we did enjoy a special relationship. I'd never thought about the consequences of this complicity, but I admit that certain situations were more than ambiguous.

Vic came to sit down again.

"The customers always want what I don't have! What bad luck. Briefly, where were we?"

"I said that my relationship with Darren couldn't be more normal."

"Really? Good. In that case, it's perfect."

He remained pensive for a short moment. I didn't know how to lie very well. He pointed it out to me.

"Say instead that you don't want to talk about it..."

"It's not true. Only, what is it that you'd like me to say? You should ask him yourself."

"I did that..."

"And?"

"He said no more than you did."

"That's because there's nothing to say."

"Then, let's say no more about it."

"Amélie told me that..."

He pretended to be scared.

"You spoke with Amélie? Brrr!!!"

"Yes, I did speak to her. She told me that vampires were curious... And as you can see, I believe her!"

He began to roar with laughter. Maybe I'd managed to divert the conversation.

The concert came to an end. As usual, the musicians chatted with their fans. I emptied my glass and went outside to wait for Darren. Strangely, I had the urge to smoke, which I did without very much pleasure.

"Didn't you like the music, this evening?" Asked Darren, who joined me very discreetly.

"Of course yes! What makes you say that?"

"You're outside, ready to leave."

"I just had the urge to smoke, but the result wasn't quite what I'd hoped for."

I flicked the butt into the gutter, disappointed. My disappointment about the cigarette made him smile. Vampires were healthy beings!

"I shall leave after the ball," I said suddenly.

"You're not obliged to."

"I know, but I have a load of things to do: Empty my apartment, the appointment with the doctor... I especially have to become used to a "normal" life again before I go back to work."

"I'll help you with that, don't worry for the moment! Organize the ball, then we'll see."

"All right, thank you."

I smiled, but something told me that those would be difficult times. Then, I looked at him with a sidelong glance, avoiding his gaze.

"Is it true that you never lend your car?"

"Yes, was Vic put out about that?"

"No, only surprised. And me, flattered!"

I activated the car's central locking and took my place again behind the steering wheel before he could change his mind. In leaning across to the passenger side to open him the door, I noticed Vic behind the window of the club. He seemed jealous.

"If you'd care to step inside, Sir?" I said in the spirit of a joke.

He complied and chose some Mozart for the return trip, which didn't make me drive any less quickly. I adored driving his sports car.

8

I visualised myself in the near future. The ball would take place in fifteen days' time. I tried to imagine this room full of people all spinning around and dancing. I sat down right in the middle of the room, on the floor, my iPod to my ears. I was full of ideas. The problem lay with verifying just what Hector had at his disposal to bring them to fruition.

I got up and went into the kitchen. He wasn't there. I found him in the gardens, right where I'd completed my transformation. He was pruning the rosebushes. As soon as he saw me, he removed his gloves.

"Hello, Miss Lilly, what may I do for you?"

"Hello Hector. I'd like to look at the furniture we can use for the ballroom. It's time for me to think about the decor."

"Of course," he said.

He put his clippers on a bench and went with an assured step towards a door situated below the steps which led to the rear of the building.

"It wasn't that urgent," I told him, catching him up.

"We store everything in this cellar. I'll let you choose in peace. Let me know if you need anything else. I shall return to the garden. And know that you didn't disturb me: What's done is done!"

This man was strange. His life was completely dedicated to Darren and to this chateau. Decidedly, he'd chosen an odd existence.

The cellar was monstrously big and, without doubt, it contained some real hidden treasures. I stayed here exploring the cellar for two hours without being able to make a decision. It was too vast, every era and style was represented here. It was impossible to choose.

I left to find Hector, I really needed his help. Now, he was pruning the shrubs. He was really patient, and certainly passionate.

"Did you find anything that you liked?"

Given my sigh of disillusionment, he understood my confusion. Next, the same ritual as two hours earlier: He removed his gloves, but this time, he sat down on a bench.

"Explain to me what you would like, maybe I can choose for you."

I took a seat alongside him, it was the first time we'd been this close.

"Thank you, because there are too many things and I wouldn't want to mix periods or to commit an error of taste. It's important, you understand?"

"Quite so, yes. Knowing that the ball will have as its theme the Victorian era, the choice of furniture will be easy. Tell me how you would like to arrange the room."

He took some pleasure in helping me, it altered his routine. I was delighted, it was a solace to me.

"We need a stage; a group will be performing, if Vic finds one, which I don't doubt. Then, a buffet. There'll be humans too... And them, they'll be dining! Chairs, naturally, and some tables. You know, I've never organised such a party and I'm a little lost. But I'd like something authentic. The room lends itself very well to this. Ah! Yes, and flowers too. But not in front of the French windows, in case the guests would like a romantic escapade in the park. Regarding the stage, ideally Vic should be asked, in order to determine its size. Do you know him?"

"Yes, I'll call him. I'd like to suggest that I deal with all of this. After what you've just explained, I'll be able to do something good. When I'm ready, together we shall see if it suits you."

"Perfect. I don't know how to thank you."

He returned my smile and stood up.

"Well, I have to finish pruning these; if it freezes, all will be lost."

"Thank you again! Even if I've said it too much, I insist!"

"You're welcome, Miss Lilly."

At least, this aspect was settled. For the moment, apart from Marie, I found vampires easy to live with, but I hadn't thought that everything would be sorted out so quickly. As a result, I no longer knew how to fill my time.

I went back into the attic to examine - or rather to admire – the dresses and find some shoes. The ascent was once again made without any breathlessness. My new physical condition still surprised me so much. To be honest, it was unhoped-for. I was in even more than great shape: I was brimming with energy. It was a real pleasure.

In the attic, the choice turned out to be just as difficult as in the cellar. My eyes only settled upon marvels. I caressed the clothes gently. But all of a sudden, a strange thing occurred when my hand settled on an orangey dress. I recoiled, perplexed. Indeed, while my hand had touched the fabric, I had the fleeting glimpse of a woman. I approached the garment anew, I grabbed it this time by the hanger and dangled it in front of me. Nothing happened. On the other hand, when I carefully placed my right hand on the shoulder of the dress, I immediately saw this woman again.

Things gradually became clearer around her. She walked along a street, a market you might say, it was a very long time ago. She was smiling, looking at the stalls. A man approached her, they seemed to know each other. He called her Agathe. At the sound of this voice, I took my hand away once again.

I was a little frightened by this discovery. Where had this gift come from? I went downstairs to the library, almost running. I had to discuss it with Darren. Him, he could explain it to me. I didn't bother to knock. He was at his desk. He raised his eyes towards me, a little surprised even so.

"Hello Lilly," he said calmly.

"Hello Darren. Tell me; something strange has just happened to me and I need an explanation."

"I'm listening," he said, settling comfortably against the back of his armchair.

"Well, I was in the attic choosing a dress, I ran my hand over all the fabrics... They're so soft, you understand? When suddenly, on touching one of them, I had a vision. I'm not crazy, believe me!"

He was watching me attentively.

"Continue. What happened next?"

"I recoiled at first, but it was so strange, so I grabbed the hanger and set it in front of me. I put my hand back on the dress and again I saw her!"

"Who?"

"A woman. She was walking along the street. I don't know in which era, but she wore that orangey dress. Have you seen the one I mean?"

"You know, there are lots of dresses up there… And what next?"

"She was walking in a market. A man approached her and called her Agathe. I immediately removed my hand, I had the feeling that I'd gone back into the life of these people. Is this another gift which you've passed on to me?"

"No, I don't possess that one, and to tell the truth, very few vampires have it. It's the gift of retrograde clairvoyance, it's very rare."

"In what way is it useful?"

"Gifts are not necessarily either useful or useless. It's up to us to use them advisedly. I admit that I haven't gone into the matter in great detail, because I don't possess this gift myself. It could turn out to be useful within the framework of a particular event which you needed information or proof about. I'm going to do some research, okay?"

"Does it represent a particular danger for me?"

"I don't believe so. Wait!"

He got up and went to one of the shelves situated near the entrance. He passed his fingers along the books, whilst he read out the titles in a low voice.

"Ah! Here we are," he said, coming back to sit down.

"You have books which explain the gifts?"

"You bought a book on the quays in Paris about vampires, why wouldn't there be one about the gifts or vampiric medicine?"

"That's true, indeed. Have you found anything?"

He raised his head and gave a suggestion of a smile.

"Not yet. You're so impatient?"

"I know, forgive me. All this is so new…"

"I've found something!" He announced proudly.

He handed me the book. A very old work written in a bizarre French.

"For you to read, Lilly, I'm here in case something isn't clear."

"All right. It looks like it's handwritten?"

"You're right and you wouldn't find it in a bookshop."

"A unique volume?"

"I think so, yes."

"Can you imagine how much work this represented? A lifetime's effort!"

I closed the book in order to read the name of the author.

"If this Artur Mills didn't possess all these gifts himself, which he describes here, he must have done years of research to have assembled everything there was in this book. Or perhaps, he was the most powerful of vampires!"

"He is very powerful and old, indeed. You are perceptive."

"Is he still alive?"

"Yes, he's retired to the mountains of Tibet, but still alive."

"How did you come to own this book?"

"It was Martin who entrusted it to me. I keep it here, but it by no means belongs to me. This book is a part of our heritage."

The incident at the club came back to my mind.

"Is this room protected against fire, at least?"

"Yes. What's more, many very rare papers are kept here. Since Amélie's misadventure, the entire chateau has a fire alarm system. This room is the pinnacle of high technology as regards its protection: Fire, flood, intrusion and naturally, theft."

"All that despite its ancient appearance."

"That's how I wanted it. Come on, what does the book say?" He asked, returning to the subject of my visit.

"Retrograde clairvoyance or seeing into the past by touching: This gift allows one to go back into a precise moment in the life of the owner of the aforementioned object. It turns out to be very useful during a trial, during a case of amnesia or simply to relive certain moments. For an experienced vampire, it will be easy to go to a very precise date; whereas for a novice, he will have a random glimpse of the life of the owner. It takes many years in order to manage this very rare gift correctly, in order to be capable of going to a desired date, particularly because of the rarity of the gift itself and, for the reason that there is little help available to a novice (5th Thermidor of the year 1799). This gift, combined with telepathy, is a major advantage for a vampire, giving them the possibility of listening to conversations, and allowing them to confirm any statements. The combination of both gifts is very rare (to this day, 10% of the vampires which I have met). That last information is written in ball-point pen, in the margin. Is it normal?"

"It's a book to be kept up to date," he explained. "But how do we go to the date of our choice?"

"There are entire pages of explanations. I'll do you a precise report, I promise!" I answered, laughing. "Hey you're becoming very curious, now!"

"What were you thinking about when this occurred?"

"I imagined myself in a ballroom, in another time. Do you believe that nothing would've happened, if I'd been thinking of something different?"

"Probably. I hope so, otherwise, you risk being bothered by this gift. Especially if you don't manage it properly."

"You're right. May I take the book to my bedroom?"

"Yes, but take good care of it!"

"Naturally. When's our second dancing lesson, Darren?"

He looked at me with an air of amazement. He hadn't expected such a question.

"I'll come and fetch you from your room. For the time being, I've some business to finish."

I stood up keeping the book carefully between my hands, such a treasure it was.

"All right, see you later."

He looked pensive. I very much hoped not to have bothered him. Since my arrival at the chateau, and following my transformation, I'd taken up a lot of his time. Ought I to make myself more discreet?

I saw that the sun had descended behind the treetops. This book was fascinating and I didn't notice the hours going by. I'd inherited a very unusual gift. I still didn't know what use I would make of it, but I wanted to practise in order to master it in case it would be useful to me one day.

Suddenly I looked up. Somebody was approaching my room... Hector. I opened the door before he knocked. I surprised him, with his hand in the air. That made him smile.

"You learn quickly, Miss Lilly."

"Thanks!"

"Sir awaits you in the ballroom. I shall be in the kitchen. If you wish to make any changes…?"

"Okay. Have you already finished arranging everything?"

"A child's game," he remarked, laughing.

This time, it was me who stood there, speechless. Hector amused me with his surprises. He seemed to have begun smiling day after day. The austere and terrifying man of the first instance, had given way to a being, both nice and full of humour.

I rushed downstairs to the ballroom. I was impatient. Things were becoming a reality at a staggering speed. I stopped at the door for a few moments to catch my breath. I sensed Darren's presence inside.

"You risk being late for your lesson, Miss!" He shouted.

From the moment that the door opened, I was immediately filled with amazement at the picture which my eyes had been offered. Hector had interpreted my ideas correctly. Despite few clues, he'd guessed at what I'd wished for. The room didn't seem so big any more, now that it was furnished.

The stage for the group was arranged against the wall at the far end, facing the entrance. For the moment, two big curtains were open on each side. On the left hand side, in front of the windows, was another stage, much smaller, scattered with a few chairs. Perhaps it would serve for the musicians during the opening waltzes? Here and there, Hector had added hangings which matched the curtains.

He'd also neatly arranged the tables almost everywhere, but still keeping a sufficiently large space for dancing. The piano was still there, it brought a special touch to the room.

I gradually ventured in further. There were so many things to see! Considering that, this morning, the room was still empty! It was magnificent. I had tears in my eyes. Drawing level with Darren, I said to him:

"Why are vampires so perfect?"

He gently tilted my face up towards him, and smiled at me.

"We aren't."

He took a handkerchief out of his pocket.

"Are you tired or in need of sleep?"

"Very funny! How come you're speaking like a human?"

"I'm human above all. It's my bit of humanity which made you what you are," he said, wiping away my tears.

"Yes, and I thank you again for it. No, I'm not tired, it's just a surplus of emotion. I've hardly been here one week, and everything which has happened to me has been so wonderful! Except maybe the episode in the park, of course..."

Yes, on proper reflection, I'd been here for only six days, but it comprised one hundred and forty four hours lived with such intensity, since the matter of not sleeping multiplied the daytime by two. I did so much in a day, I learnt many things about my circle of friends, through books and by my own experiments. Such a child, I was fascinated by this new world which was around me. Certainly, this world was still very much closed for the time being, for the sake of my safety, but why would it be any different outside?

Not only had Darren saved my life, but he'd welcomed me into his family. He pulled me away from my thoughts by taking me by the hand. The lesson could begin.

Hector had installed a sound system. I heard the first notes of a Mozart waltz. Darren didn't have to explain the steps to me again. Already, we were spinning within the immensity of the room. A closeness and a magical moment. The music carried on, we danced silently. The lesson was perfect.

I remained persuaded that Darren was a little bit nostalgic for this time. He savoured this present moment, I felt it. He was serene, but this moment of happiness was short-lived, because suddenly, he froze, listening alertly. I heard fast footsteps far off, which were approaching. Hector rushed into the room, with a grave expression.

"It's Marie!" He said.

Darren ran to meet him.

"Where is she? What happened?"

He stood facing Hector.

"How's she doing?" He asked.

"She's in Scotland, I don't have any details. They were attacked."

"Prepare the helicopter, I'll be at the aerodrome in thirty minutes. Lilly, you stay here and speak to nobody."

He'd already gone to the door, with Hector behind him.

"But..." I said, trying to follow them.

"There are no buts! Do what I tell you," he said, without turning around.

I didn't want to be ousted so easily. Much to his surprise, I grabbed his arm. He turned to face me. His look was black.

"Take me along! I can be useful to you. In the worst case, I'll support you."

He stared me right in the eye, but I didn't give in.

"As you wish," he nodded in agreement. "Hector; add Lilly to the flight plan, please."

9

We drove along very quickly and, within thirty minutes, we were at the Paris heliport. All the formalities had already been taken care of, so that we could take off.

Darren hadn't said a word since our departure. He helped me to fasten myself in, and put some headphones onto my ears. Me too, I was now in direct contact with the control tower. When he began speaking with the flight controllers, he seemed calm. Only his eyes betrayed his anxiety. What had happened in Scotland? I was still surprised that he'd accepted me being here, but I didn't want to stay on my own wandering around the chateau, without any news.

The flight to Aberdeen lasted almost three hours. Once through Customs, a car awaited us. Not a moment's respite on our journey. We headed straight away in the direction of Stonehaven, in the South. Thirty minutes would be needed to travel the eighteen miles which separated both communities. Darren knew the place well. The day got up over the Scottish countryside, the dawn over the North Sea was magnificent. It was my first visit here.

A long straight road brought us to a castle. Undeniably, vampires liked such places steeped in history. On a sign, I read the name "Dunnottar's Castle".

Marie was waiting for us at the foot of the steps. She was alone and seemed in good health. On the other hand, she'd been crying and her complexion was pallid. On seeing me, she said nothing. Our last encounter had rather been tense... Now, I was part of the family; circumstances were different. She wasn't in a strong position any longer!

Darren ran towards his sister and gave her a hug.

"What happened?" He asked straight away.

"We were attacked. Everything happened so quickly... We didn't see anything coming, I'm sorry."

"Do you know who it was?"

"Not the slightest idea. They came in, immobilised me and took Albert. I spent a great deal of time finding him. Come, I'll show you, he's in the basement. I don't understand, they had nothing to say, nothing to ask..."

Myself included, she invited us to follow her.

"What did they do to him?" I asked.

"They only overpowered him. But it's strange, you'll see..."

Her voice cracked on these words, which worried Darren.

"Lilly, I don't know if you should accompany us. Let me see what state he's in first."

"I'm here, so I'm coming with you! Don't overprotect me, please."

"All right, but stay behind me. And put your senses on alert, you never can tell!"

The atmosphere in the basement was bristling with electricity. A faint glow illuminated the far end of the room and, under an alcove, I could make out a big translucent egg. A motionless form could be seen inside. The sight of this ensemble was surreal.

I stayed behind Darren as he'd asked: I was also here to learn. We approached. Albert was laid out in the centre of this kind of cocoon, a stake planted into his body. He didn't seem to be suffering, he was simply imprisoned. Darren looked around him, in search of an opening, trying to understand. I couldn't take my eyes off this completely unreal spectacle.

"They hadn't anything to say, anything to ask? Are you sure, Marie?"

"Yes, completely. Do you believe that you can get him out from there?"

"I'm thinking about it."

He remained motionless, with a vacant expression. Then, suddenly, he came over to me, a glimmer of hope in his eyes.

"Lilly?"

"Yes?"

"Do you believe you'd be capable of using the gift that you discovered with the dress?"

"I can try. Do I have to touch the cocoon?"

"Yes."

"What gift are you talking about?" asked Marie.

"Lilly possesses the gift of retrograde clairvoyance. We only noticed it yesterday, but nothing ventured, nothing gained."

"It's a very rare gift, Lilly, lucky for us!"

She smiled.

"Let's wait to see the result. Then, we'll really know if it's lucky. I discovered it by accident and I'm far from knowing how to make the most of it."

I moved towards the cocoon, trying to remember what I'd read the day before on the subject. Its texture seemed to be sticky, I hoped it wasn't a trap. Then I began to communicate with Darren with my thoughts. With caution, because I didn't want to reveal my gift to whoever this was.

"Darren, can you read my thoughts?"

"Yes, be attentive and careful."

"I have nothing to fear...?"

After a long silence, I repeated my question:

"I have nothing to fear, right?"

"Honestly, I don't know anything about it. I've never seen such a trap. Stay on your guard, I'm near you."

He wanted to be reassuring. I turned around, he was ready to pull me back to him should any danger arise. Besides, he was ready for any eventuality. At this moment, he'd become a vampire again.

My hand trembled above the cocoon, I'd have to go back far enough in time to discern the owner of this trap, as well as their intentions. On contact it didn't feel cold, as I would have imagined.

"I'd say that it's alive... In any case, it's radiating energy, it's hot."

I'd said it out loud so that Marie didn't feel left out. In fact, I didn't know whether this information was reassuring for her. Suddenly, I established contact with the past. I was in a courtyard. Four men were talking and one of them held a miniature version of the cocoon in his hand. I tried to make out what they were saying. Alas! I didn't understand this language. The man who held the cocoon wore a long robe. This detail surprised me and immediately made me think of a wizard. The other three were dressed normally.

All of a sudden, the wizard turned his head in the direction I was watching from. I took fright. Was he able to detect my presence, now in the present? I acted on reflex to interrupt the contact, I had to speak to Darren.

I turned to him, he seemed intrigued. He couldn't - at least, so I thought - have seen the things I did, but he'd heard snatches of the conversation.

"What language was that?"

"That of the wizards..."

"Wizards? As in Harry Potter?"

The reference amused him.

"Not completely, I would say that they're more in the lineage of Merlin. Thanks to their potions, their life expectancy is approximately three hundred years and they're very similar to humans. For the most part they're peaceful, they live in a very closed community. But I don't understand: Thus far, the wizards had never helped a vampire to fight another vampire. We live in harmony with these people. Why such an alliance?"

"Did you recognise him?"

"I didn't see anything, Lilly; only sounds pass through you."

I pursued our conversation out loud, so that Marie could benefit from the information.

"There was a courtyard, in the middle of which four men were standing; three vampires and a wizard, he was holding the cocoon in his hand. They spoke, but I didn't understand them. Then, the wizard turned to look at me. Could he sense me, Darren?"

"I don't know. What did he look like?"

"Difficult to say, I'm going to go back there. Ah! Yes... His look was piercing, his irises were yellow."

"It's a characteristic of wizards."

"I'm not a great help to you, I'm afraid."

"Much more than you believe."

For the first time in some hours, he smiled at me.

"Does Albert have any contact with wizards, Marie?" He asked his sister.

"Well, there's a community not far from here, but as far as I know, he doesn't have any involvement with them."

She was surprised by his question, by the situation, the wizards, and their possible relationship to Albert.

"What activity do the wizards practise around here, Marie?"

"Most of them own shops or dispensaries."

"As for Albert, he owns an antique shop, is that right?"

"Yes, but what's the link?"

Marie was on the defensive.

"I don't know, I'm just looking for something. I can see only one hypothesis wherein a wizard becomes allied with vampires and vice versa: One asked the other for help; and we have to discover why."

While they continued their discussion, I turned back to the cocoon, because we needed more information.

This time I found myself in a bar. The wizard was talking to a man. I understood what the man was talking about, but I couldn't make head nor tail of it. I just knew that they were talking about a box.

Suddenly, I was disconnected and a voice told me:

"Don't tire yourself out looking for clues, I'm going to help you and then can you release me."

Somebody had got into my head!

"Albert?"

"Yes. Leave your hand on the cocoon and listen to me carefully."

- 150 -

In spite of his position, the tone of his voice was composed. I hoped that Darren would join me in thought. This intrusion frightened me a little, because I knew nothing about Albert. If all vampires were telepathic, why did they hide this gift? I resumed:

"*Wait... Why should I trust you?*"

"*It's I who have to trust you: You have my life in your hands. I'll answer your questions, I promise you, but before that, help me, please. It's very uncomfortable here.*"

"*Does it hurt?*"

"*Not yet, but I'm at the mercy of these people. Well? Do you agree to help me?*"

"*What must I do?*"

"*Go into my shop. In the office, you'll find a safe, the combination is 73826B. Inside, there's a box wrapped in red velvet. Take it, but don't open it. Then, go to the wizard, on Eleonor Drive, and ask for someone called Polvus. Deliver this box to him personally. After that, the spell will be lifted; at least I hope so. Then, come back here and remove this stake which is immobilising me.*"

"*Pardon...? But I've never done such a thing before!*"

I really began to panic.

"*It's quite simple, you'll see. For the time being, go to the shop. Let's do what they want, you're quite willing?*"

"*Of course.*"

I spoke proudly to Darren and Marie.

"I know what has to be done!"

They turned around towards me, quite surprised.

"How do you know?" Asked Marie, verging on aggression.

"Albert told me what to do while you were talking."

"How can you be assured that it was him?"

"We'll have the proof very quickly. Come, let's go to his shop!"

Marie remained prostrate in front of the cocoon, torn between anger and surprise. Darren approached her and put a hand on her shoulder.

"You have to trust Lilly."

"That's how it seems to me," she said with a sigh.

Ten minutes later, we were in front of Albert's shop. I got ready to get out, when Darren held me by my arm.

"Wait, let me have a look at the surrounding area first," he said, getting out of the car.

He was on the alert, he signalled to us to come. Marie opened the shop and I headed directly for the office to get to the safe, as Albert had asked. Straight away I took the box and turned around towards them.

"I have to hand over this box to someone called Polvus."

"At what address?" Asked Darren.

"Eleonor Drive, that's all Albert said."

"There's only a community there. I can confirm the address," interjected Marie.

We got back into the car in total silence. I'd no idea what was going to take place within this house, nor even whether they'd let Marie and Darren accompany me. I doubted my capacity to help Albert.

We stationed ourselves at the front door, in force. I rang the doorbell, then moved back to wait. A man opened the door and stared at us:

"Just her," he said, pointing to me.

"Darren, I can't go in there alone, help me, please."

"I can't Lilly, I'll accompany you in thought. Be careful, above all."

"Darren!!"

"Go on, we can't do anything else, believe me. If it was entirely up to me…"

I got ready to follow the man, when Marie said to me:

"Lilly, good luck and thanks!"

"Thanks Marie, that means a lot to me."

I was surprised once again by her attitude, her look was sincere. I followed the man silently, all my senses on alert. I didn't have to be unduly wary of the wizards; on the face of it, we weren't enemies. After a few minutes, he stopped and opened a door. He asked me to wait for a few moments.

"Are you are there, Darren?"

"Yes, what's happening?"

"I must wait. Is your hearing as well-developed as mine? Can you hear what's said here?"

"Yes."

A few moments later, the man reopened the door and asked me to enter. The room was big, oval, with a very high ceiling. Candles were scattered around the floor. A strange design in mosaic had been put there, centuries earlier for certain. The setting and the atmosphere were very unusual. The wizards' tastes were very different from those of the vampires. I still had my eyes glued to the work, when a man spoke to me.

"Hello Miss, you have something for me, I believe."

"Hello! If you are Polvus, indeed, I have a box for you on behalf of Albert."

He came up and scrutinised me closely. His look disturbed me, I had the feeling that he was sounding me out.

"Why a wizard-spell on a vampire?" I asked, trying to divert his attention.

"For a young vampire, you're not frightened."

"You aren't my enemy. Why should I be afraid of you?"

"Quite right, we're rather peaceful people."

He flashed me a smile. This wasn't a bad man. So then, why such an action? The affront must have been strong. I held the box out to him, which he took delicately. He raised his eyes up towards me and continued:

"Before becoming a vampire, Albert was one of us."

"And?"

"He left with an object which belonged to our community and which we had to get back. Before coming to the extreme action of yesterday, we'd already asked Albert to return this box. For some obscure reason, he's refused to do so for years. In any event, it belongs to us. And now, thanks to you, we have it back."

He slid the box into the pocket of his long robe.

"Why ask vampires for help? Aren't your spells powerful enough?"

My question was spontaneous, sincere. I knew nothing about wizards, and still so little about vampires.

"Not against a vampire, no, it was necessary to immobilise him first."

"I understand. Is he free, now?"

"He will be by the time you return. The rest will be in your hands."

He took my hands in his, I observed them, then raised my eyes up towards him.

"Why mine?"

"The person who breaks the spell has to remove the stake. We built the trap like that. As a security measure."

"The vampires won't oppose it?"

"You ought to know that better than I, but their part of the affair only involved the placing of the stake. The only purpose was to get back this box, essential to our community. I have to leave you, now. Excuse us to Albert, but we had no other choice."

With these words, he turned his back to me and left the room. The other man brought me back to the door and murmured:

"Take care of yourself, miss."

"Thanks."

I was relieved to get back outside, the meeting had gone very well. Marie and Darren were waiting for me in the car, I knew that they knew everything. Pointless giving them a report. These gifts were precious.

We took the route back to release Albert silently. He was there, motionless but freed from the cocoon: The wizard had kept his promise. I approached him, with a worried look. So I got hold of him, frozen there, with the stake in his chest.

"Position yourself above him; you must remove the stake vertically," Darren told me.

"Easy to say!"

I didn't feel able to do it. Nevertheless, it was necessary. Albert looked at me, begging me to do it. I got my breath back, and then put my hands on each side of the object. Darren came to squat down in front of me, his presence reassured me. He gave me a nod. I lost myself in his eyes, his look was penetrating and it gave me strength. The extraction was done in an instant, much more easily than I would have believed. Albert's expulsion of breath was such that I was thrown backwards and I banged my head violently against the wall. He was free, alive! I threw the stake far away, it didn't bear the slightest trace of blood. Marie rushed to embrace Albert. It was ended.

Darren helped me to pick myself up. A real relief came over me. A few minutes later, we found ourselves around a glass and some well-deserved capsules. Albert needed strength.

He explained his story to us, that he was still a wizard, and guardian of this box for many years. He wanted to keep this position, but alas, it wasn't possible in the eyes of his old community! Nobody did anything about it until now. Next, Albert was going to have to explain himself to Marie. If she'd known about his past, it would have made things easier. She wouldn't have needed us!

Darren got up. For us, it was time to return. Albert hugged me, thanked me once again and added that I'd been brave. Marie did the same. For the first time since my transformation, I felt exhausted.

Darren took the coastal road. The landscape was lavish even at night, the fresh air on my face did me good. I'd accomplished my first action of survival and help as a vampire. I'd retained my generous side to others, and this acknowledgement delighted me. I would be a good vampire! I put my hand on Darren's, I so greatly needed this warmth which we emanate.

The flight took place without a hitch, I rested and I was happy to be back at the chateau.

10

I got up with the strange sensation of having rested, as if I'd really sunk into sleep, which couldn't be the case, as far as I knew. I very much doubted it though. I went into the bathroom: My eyes were puffy. So perhaps I had indeed slept? How was it possible?

Very few things amazed me nowadays. I stored this fact away in a corner of my mind and went out to get some fresh air in the park.

After ten minutes walking alongside the hedges, which had been perfectly maintained by Hector, I came across a clearing. A surprising discovery, because nobody took care of that side of the property. I crossed it. It seemed immense to me, for a very good reason: It was the bank of a lake which I hadn't been able to see; the grasses were so high.

Some birds were coming in to land on the water, I regretted not having brought my camera. I did miss photography, I liked immortalising moments like this one.

The view over this lake was magnificent, I'd made a beautiful discovery. Everything here was peaceful. I decided to lie down on the grass, to look at the sky. Decidedly, this November was very mild. Unless it was my colder body giving me this impression, difficult to tell… The sky was very blue, scattered with a few clouds. A light breeze made the tall grasses ripple around me, this rustling relaxed me. I fully appreciated this peace of mind.

The only downside for me was that I couldn't understand this night's sleep. This detail ceaselessly came back into my mind. I closed my eyes to take best advantage of this privileged moment of communion with nature.

"Scotland was a tough ordeal for you, Lilly?"

I jumped, I hadn't heard him arrive. I sat up on my elbows, tilted my head backwards and saw Darren standing just behind me. From this angle he looked much taller.

"You scared me... Hello Darren."

"Hello Lilly."

"More interesting than tough, Darren. Enriching also: I learnt a lot about vampires, wizards too, their existence. I even learnt how to surpass some of my limitations. I did well to accompany you, don't you believe?"

"Yes, of course. It was fortunate that you were there. We would certainly have been able to solve the problem, but it would've taken much more time. What are you doing here so early in the morning?"

"I was walking and I ended up here. What a surprise to find this place!" I exclaimed with a smile.

"Yes, rather wild, compared with the rest of the park. Amélie doesn't like water, so it's uncultivated here."

"Is there is a reason for it?"

"I have no idea."

He came to sit down beside me and began throwing little pebbles into the water. What an ordinary thing to do! He did sometimes surprise me. I watched him, wondering how often he'd come here and how many times he'd actually sat here to think.

"I slept, Darren, really slept."

He turned his head towards me, with an inquiring look.

"I don't want to become human again!"

"There's no risk of that."

"Why then did I sleep?"

"What happened in Scotland exhausted you. You needed to nap more deeply, which gave you the sensation of having slept. We don't sleep Lilly, it's a known fact!"

"Well, I did, yes! I'm certain of it. My eyes were puffy."

"Very well then! I'll speak to Martin about it, stop worrying. You woke up, that's what counts, right?"

"It's true."

"Don't get stuck over details, Lilly, you'll spoil your new life."

"You're right, forgive me."

"Don't apologise!"

On these words, we were left in a fit of giggles, even though there was nothing funny. That relieved the tension, this place was perfect for that. I lay down on the grass once again, Darren did likewise.

"Is everything ready for the ball?" He asked.

"Yes, your friends helped me a lot. I've been lucky."

I smiled, but he couldn't see it.

"I've already said it, but they love you!"

"Maybe you're right. I'm looking forward to Saturday impatiently."

"Is it worrying you?"

"A little, yes. Are the guests going to come? Will the musicians be up to it? And me, will I know how to honour you?"

"I don't doubt that for an instant!"

He turned his head towards me, took my hand, squeezed it and added:

"Really!"

He'd thought about what he said, I saw it in his eyes. Eyes never lie. Right now, his look was very gentle, and proud at the same time. He was proud of my performance in Scotland, proud that I was able to make a success of that ordeal. I could feel it.

"Did you choose your dress?"

"No, but I have some idea."

"We could choose it together? Before my departure this evening…"

I turned abruptly to him.

"What departure?"

"I'm leaving for Italy, it's the meeting of the chieftains. We meet every two years to review and discuss recent events."

"You're leaving me here on my own?"

"I can't take you along this time, I'm sorry. But you won't be alone: There's Hector, Amélie… Besides, you've still got a load of things to do for the ball."

"But I'm going to be bored! I'm not used to being alone. If anybody comes, what am I supposed to do?"

"Nothing, that's Hector's role. Don't worry, I'll be back soon and everything will be all right."

He smiled, but I didn't return his smile. I was frightened by the idea of staying here on my own and I couldn't even tell him that I was going to miss him.

He got up and offered me his hand.

"Come, we're going to choose your dress. It'll be another thing that's done, and then I'll know how I'll be dressing myself."

"If you want," I said sadly.

I took his hand grudgingly. We were face to face right now, but I didn't dare look at him.

"Lilly?"

I raised my eyes towards him.

"Yes, Darren?"

"Don't be sad, it's only for a few days. I really can't take you along."

"I could look around the city during your meetings, for example... Do a little tourism. I've never been to Italy."

"No Lilly, not this time."

"Don't you trust me enough?"

"It's not a question of trust: I don't want anything to happen to you. You don't know Italy and I don't want to leave you just like that, alone, in an environment that's unknown to you. You understand?"

"No, but I haven't any choice."

I resigned myself to it. This time, I knew that I couldn't convince him.

"I'll take you there another time, when I've time to devote to you."

"All right. Let's go and choose this dress. What time are you leaving?"

"At about 10pm. We still have plenty of time!"

I hinted at a slight smile, I felt sad at the idea of him leaving, even for a few days. I ought to get used to being far away from him anyway, because I lived many kilometres from here. When I returned to my human life, I'd have to do it. I was really dreading this moment.

I was lost in my thoughts. I was quite surprised to find myself at the door.

"Don't think about it anymore, it'll be over quickly. And then, you'll be free of me just a little, which will do you good."

I walked past him without a look.

"Do you believe so?"

"Lilly!" He sighed, following me.

I looked at the dresses, but my heart wasn't in it. I tried to pull myself together. A magnificent purple dress attracted my attention.

"Would this one please you, Darren?"

He came over to me, with a sad look. Maybe I'd been a little bit harsh.

"It's magnificent! Put it on, so that I can see you."

"No, you'll have that surprise on the day of the ball," I answered, teasing him.

"That's not fair!"

"I know!"

Presently, I went over to the jewellery. There was a big choice in the display cabinets. I had my nose almost stuck to the glass, I was full of admiration at so many marvels. I pointed to a set made from sapphires.

"I like those, what do you think about them?"

"We wouldn't see them, you'd need something more sparkly."

I watched him scrutinising the display cabinet, he was looking for something very specific. He opened the doors, and put his hands on a necklace containing a single ruby.

"Here's what I'm thinking of," he said, placing it around my neck.

I looked in the mirror and put my hands on the jewel. It was very beautiful, indeed.

"It does sparkle, you're right."

I turned to him so he could admire me.

"Yes, it's perfect! Very good choice Lilly," he said, giving me a wink.

"But…"

He put his hand over my mouth and whispered:

"Hush! It's a very, very good choice."

"Thanks for your help Darren. Now, I'll need some shoes."

"I would prefer it yes, in case I unexpectedly tread on your feet."

I roared with laughter: If there was ever somebody to tread on another person's feet, it was me!

"How kind you are, Darren!"

"I know. Here's what I have to offer you."

He showed me; not just a few, but hundreds of pairs of shoes. He didn't know how to do things by half, everything was like that in the chateau. The choice was more extensive than in a shop.

"This place would turn the head of any fashion victim. Are you aware of that?"

"Of course."

I looked at him, with an air of disillusionment. He was very sure of himself. I was ready to thump him, but I decided otherwise. This gesture would maybe have been inappropriate, under the circumstances. I chose a pair of black court shoes, they suited me, it was all perfect.

"Here we are, I believe that nothing else is missing. That was quick, in the end."

"Yes, you're ready for the ball."

"And you, how will you be dressed?"

"You'll see on the day of the ball. I too, have to keep my little secrets."

He flashed me a big smile. I'd deserved it, after all.

On these words, we went back down to have some coffee in the big room. Time flew by very quickly. Already, the day was ending.

"Will you will call me to let me know that you got there?"

"If you wish, but nothing will happen to me, you know."

"I'd feel better if you did. Please..."

"All right. During my absence, if anything abnormal happens, advise me immediately. Don't try to solve any problems on your own."

"Okay."

"Promise me," he insisted.

I looked at him, he was being serious.

"I promise you."

"I must leave now," he said, getting up.

"Already? You told me 10pm."

"I'm taking a commercial flight. By the time I get to Orly, check in my luggage..."

"Can I take you to the airport?"

"No, Vic will do it."

I lowered my head, I didn't feature at all in his plan. Then, he knelt down before me and took my hands. Smiling to me, he kissed them.

Hector entered the room, Darren went over to him.

"Watch over Lilly," he whispered without me missing a word.

"Safe journey, Darren."

"Thank you Lilly!"

He could hear my words without me speaking them, we could be in contact all the time. With that, I left, to rest in my bedroom. I was thinking about what I was going to do for the next few days, alone or almost so, in this big chateau.

11

This time, I hadn't slept, just drowsed. I was feeling sad to be practically alone here. These few days were going to seem very long to me, because I had no car. I was trapped between the chateau, the gardens and the lake. There were worse places to be captive, but I felt imprisoned all the same. I was lost in my thoughts, when someone knocked on my door. Apart from Hector, who could it be? In any case, their scent wasn't known to me.

"Lilly?"

I recognised Amélie's voice. What was she coming for? I got up and opened the door.

"Hello, Amélie."

"Do you want to accompany me up to the greenhouse to choose the flowers for Saturday?"

"Of course! One moment, I'll get a pullover."

She looked at the bedroom, as if this part of the chateau was completely unfamiliar to her.

"Did Darren ask you to occupy me somehow?"

"Not at all. He never spoke to me."

This last sentence surprised me.

"Why not?"

She didn't answer. It was pointless to keep on trying.

"Let's go," I said to her, smiling.

I'd still kept the book about the gifts. I'd have to read the part concerning the gift of double clairvoyance which Amélie possessed.

We crossed the park by its left hand side; her dog came to join us. Apparently, Amélie's movements around the property were more free and easy when Darren was absent.

Like everything else here, the greenhouse was gigantic. The dome was made from glass, in the traditional way. Certain stained-glass windows depicted flowers; hand-painted, without doubt. I went up and down the rows, nourished by numerous scents and colours, when my gaze came to rest on a lily.

"What variety of flower is this?"

Amélie came back over to me and delicately touched the petals. Unlike the first time I'd met her, her face was very relaxed. We were in her territory, she felt good here and it showed.

"A black lily," she eventually answered.

"I didn't know such a thing existed. How do you know it's black?"

The question just slipped off my tongue. For a fraction of a second, I felt something worse than just a look upon me. I'd asked a question which wasn't necessary, I'd been tactless.

Now, she knew that I knew. She answered me quite naturally:

"Due to its texture. It's a hybrid and very rare. For years, we've been trying with lilies. It's the second time that we've succeeded. The result isn't perfect yet, but we're getting close."

Knowing her handicap, this amazed me.

"You did it yourself?"

"Along with Hector. It's our passion. I'll show you… We were featured in an article on the greenhouse and our work in several magazines, such as "Gardens magazine". If that's of interest to you, of course."

"That would be nice, yes."

I had some time before Darren would return. I could therefore linger over Amélie's flowers and so get to know her a little as well. She showed me the greenhouse, it was wonderful and completely undetectable from the outside. I hadn't even noticed this magnificent building. You could find all sorts of flowers, house plants and even cacti here. It'd taken a lot of time. She was passionate about it and had received quite a lot of awards, not only for her diverse research, but for the greenhouse itself, its beauty and its upkeep. Amélie lived her own life in this chateau. But the only thing which linked her with Darren, was her husband Hector.

I returned to the chateau and went instinctively to the ballroom. I settled down at the piano, looked at the keyboard, then at my hands, which I delicately placed on the keys. My fingers began playing Sarah McLaghan's "Possession". Again, the music filled the room and the magic worked.

My spirit wandered, I missed Darren. Something I couldn't divulge to anyone. My fingers slid along the keyboard, the keys danced beneath their touch. My eyes misted over. Darren, the music… I loved this state. I didn't know what affected me most. Maybe it formed a whole, a carefully balanced mixture between the music and Darren's aura? I was previously unable to play the piano this well, this gift had come from Darren. Nevertheless, it wasn't anything vampiric.

My gaze was riveted to the French window, in front of me. Outside, the wind had got up, I could see the trees bending with its gusts. November had well and truly settled in. The spectacle was enchanting.

The few leaves which the late autumn had overlooked, were spinning uncontrollably under the influence of the wind. Some made their way into the room and came over to die near the piano. The spectacle was surreal.

Suddenly, a flash of lightning brought me back to reality and I saw a figure cross my field of vision. Furtive, rapid... I stopped playing immediately, but the danger didn't restore my human appearance. I got up and arrived at the window without even being aware of it: I was that fast. I scrutinised the gardens, all my senses on the alert, and glanced over towards Hector's house; they were sleeping.

I didn't dare to go out. Darren had told me to call him, most of all not to brave the danger alone. What should I do? It was night-time and he was so far away...

I chose the option of closing the window. At least, I wasn't at any risk inside the chateau. I went to my bedroom, I got the book about the gifts and left, taking refuge in the most secure room in this place: The library. Maybe I'd call him tomorrow to tell him what I'd seen.

I spent the night reading the book, I had so much to learn, and watching outside. But nothing moved, except the trees under the force of the wind. I couldn't see the figure any longer and I told myself that maybe I'd dreamt about it, which I doubted strongly, because my eyes had become very effective, especially in the darkness. It was so fast that it could only have been a vampire or a creature I didn't know anything about. The memory was very real, so I concluded that it was true.

In the early hours, I went out to look at the extent of any damage. The wind had calmed down and had left the place with an icy air which suited me. On the ground, there were only leaves; the smallest of the shrubs hadn't made it through the storm.

Suddenly, I became very concerned. I quickly turned towards the greenhouse; from here, it seemed intact. I boldly headed over towards that immense building, hoping that nothing had happened to it. I had a good look around. Everything seemed to be in order, but I'd only known the place since yesterday. In any case, no fragments of glass were strewn around and the doors were closed.

Inside also, everything seemed in its place. I was relieved, I could go back to inspecting the gardens, maybe find a clue to explain my vision of last night. The frost might have preserved some tracks.

I returned to look closely at the window, and spotted the exact place where the figure had passed. I put all my senses into action and went over to the trees. Apart from the debris, which almost formed a carpet, there was nothing particular here, other than this peppery smell which was unknown to me, but didn't belong here. I followed its trail which led me near the lake, right where I'd spoken with Darren a few days earlier. The smell stopped there. Maybe the figure had crossed the river to confuse a pursuer, as it was doing to me now?

I abandoned my searching and headed back towards the chateau, ready to help Hector clean the gardens; He went to a lot of trouble to do it! The cleaning, by the three of us, lasted all day long. Hector told me that we now had some wood for winter, but I remembered inadvertently that I wouldn't be a part of that "we"... In a few days, all this would be over. He confirmed to me that the greenhouse hadn't been damaged, contrary to what had happened during the terrible storm of 1999. The structure was solid, built to last and to endure all the worst weathers.

At about six o'clock, Hector came to me with some very hot milky coffee, which was well-deserved. He thanked me for my help and told me that I could now attend to my own affairs. The majority of the work having being done, he could now finish it over the next few days. I took the coffee with pleasure and decided to slip into a bath. Another day had passed. Soon, Darren would be back. This too warmed my heart.

The bath did me a world of good, both physically and mentally. I managed to count up to six hundred and fifty underwater, but I kept my eyes open so as not to lose myself, as Darren had recommended. After a good hour, my skin had softened sufficiently for me to understand that now was the time to drag myself out of my ice-cold bath.

I put on the night-dress from the first day, the one which had made me so uneasy, and got into my bed, which seemed cosier than usual. The day's exercise had physically tired me out, a strange sensation which I hadn't felt for a long time.

I fell into our half-sleep within a few seconds and dreamed for the first time. It was a strange dream about Italy - where I'd never set foot - about the figure, the music and the wind. Everything had come together tonight in my subconscious to become a nightmare. I awoke at around 8am, sweating and feverish, and found it impossible to get up. I must've caught a cold the day before, from spending the day outside in the cold. Our body-temperature didn't allow me to judge if it was cold. Apparently, in future, I ought to pay this more attention.

Suddenly, somebody knocked on my door, I tried to sit up so as to appear to be in less of a bad way.

"Come in," I shouted, as best as I could.

"Are you going to lie in bed all day?" A familiar voice called out.

"Darren! When did you get back?"

He entered the room and came to sit down on the edge of the bed. His smile gave way to a worried look.

"But you're ill, Lilly!"

"I must have caught a cold while helping Amélie and Hector yesterday in the park. We were hit by a terrible storm, you know!"

He put his hand on my forehead and brushed aside my hair which had become stuck from the fever.

"Yes, Hector told me about the damage."

At this point, he rang the bell.

"We must restore your health quickly for the ball!" He told me.

"Yes I know. I didn't do it deliberately, forgive me. I'm happy to see you. I missed you," I told him in a murmur.

He kissed my boiling-hot forehead and pulled the blanket up under my chin.

"I missed you too!"

"Did your meeting go well?"

"Boring, as usual, but necessary."

Hector entered the room and gave me a look of surprise.

"Ask Martin to come as soon as possible, Hector."

Hector left without answering.

"It's just a nasty cold, Darren, I don't need a doctor. Tomorrow, it won't be noticeable any longer."

"Vampires never catch a cold, Lilly!" He answered gravely.

"Well I have, yes! I slept as well, and I dreamed too."

"Pardon? You dreamed?" He asked, really amazed.

"Yes, last night. I dreamt about Italy, then about this figure…"

I'd spoken too fast.

"What one, Lilly? What are you hiding from me?"

"I'm talking about my dream Darren!"

"Admittedly… Carry on."

I recounted my dream to him, such as I could remember.

"We're not supposed to dream Darren?" I asked at the end of my tale.

"If you dream, it's because you sleep, and that, we aren't supposed to do."

"Why not?"

"That's just how it is. Imagine our vulnerability while asleep!"

"Yes, but it is possible. It's just that you forbid yourselves from doing it."

"Perhaps you're right, but it worries me to know that you're vulnerable."

"How could I prevent myself from sleeping, if my body needs it and nothing worries me enough to remain vigilant?"

"I don't know, your purity as a vampire has to be at the origin of this matter."

"I'm still a young vampire," I answered, amusedly.

Martin quickly entered the room. He greeted Darren and came to my bedside. He examined me and concluded that in effect I'd caught a cold the day before, a good old human cold. Something in me had stayed how it was before; I was capable of catching illnesses. Was the illness stronger than my new condition? We'd done the transformation to avoid this, why hadn't it worked as well as it should have done? Why, even as a vampire, was I different?

Martin thought about the best remedy to put me back on my feet. He gave me a blood test, then he took Darren's left wrist and held it out to me. I watched what he was doing without understanding.

"Bite him!" He said.

Darren was as surprised as I was by the turn of events.

"I can't do that," I cried, turning my head away.

"Do as you're told, Lilly, it'll do you good, it's like a transfusion," Darren, who had now understood, said calmly.

I delicately took his wrist and caressed it. Seeing my concern, he smiled at me. He completely trusted Martin. Without asking any more questions, I gently sunk my teeth into his flesh. I felt a warm rush flowing into my body, running into the complex network of my blood system. The effect wasn't immediate, but almost so. My strength returned. Darren gave me the poison which would save me, for the second time in only a few weeks. He delicately touched my head to let me know to stop now. He wiped dry his wound, raised his eyes towards me and smiled at me again. I was horrified by my action once again.

"Am I going to have to regenerate regularly, Darren?"

He turned to Martin, who was more able to answer. He stared at me, embarrassed.

"Maybe I'll know more after the analysis of your very special blood. Sorry not to be more sure of myself, Lilly."

"Okay, let's wait. I already feel much better. Thank you, Darren."

"Did you get more tired than usual, over the last few days?" Asked Martin.

"No, apart from cleaning the garden yesterday, nothing exceptional."

"Any more transformations?"

"No. Ah! Yes, but only one: The evening of the storm."

I looked at Darren.

"Why this transformation?" He questioned.

"I was playing the piano, you know me..."

"You have to control yourself!" He shouted.

"I was alone in the chateau... You said that I was safe here."

I remained pensive, recollecting that figure. But I stayed silent for a bit too long, lost in my thoughts, which didn't escape Darren's notice.

"What happened, besides the storm?" He started again.

"Eh?"

He brought me out of my thoughts, but no lie came into mind. I carried on with my tale.

"I was playing the piano. The storm was violent, but it wasn't cold. I'd left the French windows open in front of me, it was magical. Then, there was a flash of lightning and I saw it."

I stared fixedly at Darren. He seemed frightened, he stood up and grabbed me by shoulders to make me react.

"Come back among us, Lilly. What did you see through the window and what did you do?"

"Nothing, I didn't do anything, you'd told me not to take any action. I saw a figure passing very quickly, not far away. I didn't go out, I just closed the window and went to your office to make myself safe, just in case."

"Did you tell Hector about it, as I'd asked?"

"No, they were sleeping. I didn't want to worry anybody. Then, yesterday morning, I went out to where I'd seen it, but there was nothing, except for a peppery smell. I followed the trail up as far as the lake. The figure must have crossed it to hide the trail, I think."

"When you're better, you can show me," he concluded.

"Give me a few minutes and I'll show you. I'm feeling good and I need a breath of fresh air."

They left the room and Martin went away with my blood. Darren waited for me in the ballroom. I joined him, having put on some jeans and a very warm pullover. He was looking outside, his hands behind his back.

"I had told you to alert me if something abnormal happened!"

He was more worried than angry.

"It was just the day before yesterday, Darren. Maybe I'd imagined this figure, there was so much wind..."

I stayed a few steps behind him.

"Yes, but the smell didn't invent itself!" He retorted, turning towards me. "Show me, if you want to?"

I put my hand on the door-handle, when he grabbed my arm. I turned around, frightened. He stared at me silently. It lasted for several minutes, which didn't reassure me. I would've preferred words rather than this heavy silence.

"I have understood, Darren. Please, say something! This silence is unbearable, and you're scaring me."

"It's not a game, we have many predators outside. Believe me, and in future, do what I ask you to do."

"Yes, Darren."

My answer was sincere, I sensed his concern. This time, I opened the door and headed to the place where I'd seen the figure. Darren smelt the air. He confirmed the peppery smell and followed the trail. This brought him to the lake, as it had for me. My senses were not so bad, after all.

"Do you know what it was…Or who it was?" I asked.

"It's impossible to say. If somebody uses pepper, it's because they don't want to be recognised."

He was concerned.

"Or maybe a man who got lost in the storm," he added.

"In the park? It's private here, how would he have entered?"

"Over here! The other bank of the lake isn't part of this property, it's a natural boundary," he stated.

"It's necessary to be good swimmer, then."

"Or to have a boat… What follows next, we shall see…"

I tried to reassure him:

"You see, there wasn't enough here to call you!"

"Time will tell… Quick, let's return to the warmth, Hector's going to prepare us something: I want you on top form for your ball."

"Of course," I said, on the way back to the chateau.

We settled ourselves down on the ground floor. The crackling of the fire in the fireplace brought a particular warmth to the moment. Darren stayed silent; for him, this incident hadn't been at all insignificant. Together with my health, it was enough to spoil his return.

The days which followed were dedicated to the final preparations for the ball. Excitement reigned in the chateau. I felt normal once again; that's to say vampire.

12

I was finishing my make-up. My face had changed since my transformation. I hadn't really given it any attention until today. My skin was white, perhaps a little more so than beforehand, but it was neat, clean. All the marks left on my face by my stroke had disappeared.

I chose pastel colours for the outline of my eyes. They had always been green, but much more almond-green. Formerly, they changed with the weather; now, only the transformations changed them. I'd put my hair up into a bun, letting a few locks fall here and there. They had darkened, but maybe this was due to the lighting in the room. I knew why vampires seemed so beautiful: It was because of the contrast of colours. The reflection which the mirror sent back pleased me. Everything pleased me since I'd become a vampire. This was the life for me, I adored it. Even if this life of luxury was soon going to come to an end, it would remain engraved in me forever.

I made an assessment of these last weeks and I could only see the positive there. I'd totally erased the difficult times, keeping only the best. Too bad if it wasn't the wisest of solutions: I lived, I breathed and, chiefly, I felt good, as never before. I'd lived twenty-four years of a life full of suffering, and only a few weeks of boundless vitality. I wouldn't consider going back to how it was, not for anything in the world. I'd chosen well, definitely! The choice of a different life, but a life lived one hundred percent. All this, I owed to Darren, the most beautiful encounter of my life. No exaggeration. This success had gone beyond all my expectations. I'd been resuscitated. What a paradox because, in a way, I'd half died!

He knocked on my door. One last look in the mirror then I stood up to join him. The time had come for us to welcome our guests and to open the ball.

"Are you ready?" He asked.

He behaved like a true gentleman. I opened the door and let him discover me.

I was wearing the dress which we'd chosen together. It was made from purple velvet, very light, arched up to the waist by the addition of a corset, as were the dresses of this period, and finished with petticoats; some of velvet, some of lace. The sleeves finished a little below the elbow, and worn of course with short gloves. He'd picked me a necklace set with a single ruby, with matching earrings. The set, while being simple, was very beautiful.

"You're magnificent, Lilly!" He said sincerely.

His eyes sparkled.

"Thank you, you're very handsome too."

He was wearing a black suit, which would have gone with anything, I must admit, but he'd matched his tie with my dress and had added a set pin, also of a single ruby.

He offered me his left hand, I smiled to him and placed my hand on his arm, as was proper in this period. He was my partner for my first ball.

"I have butterflies in my stomach!"

"It doesn't show in the least, you're resplendent."

He looked me over once again.

"Really!" He resumed, aiming to convince me.

Descending the stairs proved delicate. I had to pay attention to my dress, hold my head upright, and take care not to fall. Having reached halfway down, I became aware of the guests waiting in the anteroom outside. I paused awhile.

He looked at me, smiling.

"Come, Lilly, trust me."

"Yes," I answered with a sigh.

They had come! My God; the room was swarming with people. As we moved forward, they began to fall silent and to move apart. I was very impressed, we were the hosts and we should be the first ones into the room. I felt everybody's gaze upon us, I tried to smile, looking from left to right. They were all in costume. They'd all played the game! Could I conclude from this that they'd accepted me?

Hector opened the doors and let us into the room, which seemed suddenly small to me, seeing how many people were here.

According to protocol, we should stay by the entrance to welcome our guests. A classical music ensemble was already playing quietly so we could answer the people who greeted us. Fortunately, most did it more by gestures than words. It lasted an eternity. Then, Hector closed the doors, the ball could begin.

Darren led me to the centre of the room, I looked at him so as not to falter. He smiled at me, then invited me to dance our first waltz in public. I was hoping his private tuition had been enough. Apparently, yes. First one couple joined us, then two, and so on, until I was able to see nothing more than petticoats flying. It was magnificent.

"Where did you learn to waltz so well?" Asked Darren by way of a joke.

"Very funny! Don't distract me, or you might feel a little less proud of your pupil," I answered in the same tone. "Who's that dancing with Martin?"

Marie was second into the ball, then Martin. Soon, I couldn't even distinguish them all.

"Philly, I believe. I don't know her very well, she doesn't live here."

"His partner?"

"If they start a third waltz together, I would say so, yes."

"Why?"

"Two waltzes are the maximum which a lady in society can grant to a man if they're not together."

"I didn't know."

"I suspected that, which is why I explained it to you."

We started the second waltz, it was faster than the first one. I began counting again so as not to lose my step. I'd never been good at dancing. I liked music, but moving along with it was a bit difficult for me. The more the piece progressed, the more the rhythm sped up. It was becoming really hard for me. It was a relief to hear the final notes.

"I have to leave you for a moment," he told me, at the end of the waltz.

"Right now?"

"Yes, trust me!"

I looked all around me; they seemed to be having fun. The ball was going very well. It made me happy to see them like this. Everyone, without exception, had come dressed in period clothes. Philly started her third waltz with Martin: I had my answer.

I headed to the bar and took a glass of champagne, I was feeling thirsty. I didn't see Darren. I was circulating among the guests, saying hello here and there, when the third waltz ended. Somebody could be heard tapping on a microphone to check that it was working.

"Good evening to you all!"

I turned around: I'd found Darren. He'd removed his jacket and was standing on the stage. I moved closer, like the rest of the audience, to listen to him speaking.

"Rest reassured, I'm not going to sing this evening. Actually, that's not completely true: I'm going to sing one single song, then I'll make way for a real singer," he said, laughing. "This evening, here for us, is the group 'Intensity!'"

The curtain opened to reveal a group which I didn't know. A thunderous applause filled the room while Darren replaced the microphone in its stand, and while the music started. Vic was on the guitar, I didn't know he could play!

On just the first few notes, I recognised the song. I looked at them, very surprised. Darren was singing, and what's more, it was Rock! My God, how well it suited him! I couldn't take my eyes off him.

"He's changed a lot, lately," Marie said to me.

She'd appeared from nowhere, as was her habit to do. We were side by side. I was captivated by Darren's performance.

"I don't know about that," I answered politely.

"I've never seen him act like this with somebody. Never seen him taking so many risks, having so much commitment to one person. With you, he lowers his guard."

"Why are you telling me that? What guard?"

I frowned. What did Marie want with me?

"Look at him! Listen to him!"

"They're the lyrics of the song, he's just singing it. What's wrong with that?"

"Nothing's wrong, he's singing it for someone, don't you feel it?"

Yes, I did feel it. And this someone, it was me. This was his surprise.

"Darren was a powerful vampire because he was solitary," she added.

"Was...?"

"He's become vulnerable. Are you listening to me?"

I was completely hypnotized by Darren. He was addressing himself to me, it was palpable. She was right. Why did she want to spoil this moment for me?

"To tell the truth, I am listening; to him! He sings so well!"

I looked at her for an instant, to be sure I'd not angered her again. But no, she smiled at me.

"Do you know how long it's been since there was a ball in the chateau?"

"No. This ball, it was my idea. He didn't organise it for me, if that's what you're insinuating. On the other hand, this song he's singing, this wasn't planned. Not by me, in any case."

She grabbed my shoulders, trying to make me react. I stared deeply into her eyes without any fear this time, and I said:

"I'm leaving tomorrow, Marie! Calm down, you're going to get your brother back."

There was sadness in my voice as I was telling her this truth. I became conscious of it.

"Why?"

"I have to go back to work, back to my apartment, back to the world of human beings. That was the deal, Marie."

"Does he know this?"

"Of course."

"What did he say?"

"This song, isn't this his answer?"

I fixed her right in the eye, at the very moment Darren sang "Please stay", one of the final lines of "Careless Whispers".

"Don't leave him, Lilly, please."

I turned around, surprised; she was sincere. Then, I headed resolutely over towards the platform. Arriving in front of him, I offered him my hand, waiting for him to come down and join me. He took it and embraced me delicately for a dance. I put my head in the hollow of his shoulder and closed my eyes. Nobody could steal this moment away from me.

At the end of the first piece that the band played, Darren gently moved apart from me. He looked tenderly at me.

"Thank you for the song and the dance," I said to him.

"You liked it? I'm not used to singing, I felt nervous."

"The performance was perfect, the emotion intact. You should do it more often."

Even though Marie had tried to divert my attention, I had felt the song.

"Are you thirsty?" He asked.

"Yes, a little."

We went over to the bar, when a blast of coldness filled the room. Somebody had opened the door, a latecomer. Suddenly, I felt a tension in the air. People moved apart to allow the surprise guest to pass, who was coming straight towards us, then resumed their dancing. Darren moved me to his side, to protect me.

"Good evening Alexandre," he said coldly.

"Good evening Darren. I'm a little late, excuse me," he answered with a sarcastic tone.

I shifted forwards a little to see this Alexandre. He didn't resemble the other vampires, he frightened me. His face had no beauty; he had very short blonde hair, and was dressed in leather. He seemed violent and nasty. He didn't belong here. Why was he here? He turned his head to me, he had the eyes of a snake. I stepped back quickly.

"Won't you introduce me? You won't be able to hide her indefinitely, Darren!"

He smiled at me. I got a glimpse of his canines. This vampire didn't hide himself!

"Lilly, I present to you; Alexandre," said Darren reluctantly.

I was ready to hold my hand out to him, an old human reflex, but I immediately changed my mind. I didn't want him to touch me.

"Hello," I said, simply.

"Hello, pretty lady," he said with a bow.

I was really frightened. What did he want from me? It seemed very much as if he was here because of me.

"Everybody's talking about this transformation. I believed that your family didn't transmute any more, Darren? Would reason have been swept away after so many years? "

He took a glass which had been left near to him. He was bad-mannered. He drank it in one gulp, noisily.

"No Alexandre, as I said, it's none of your business."

"You found her attractive and you convinced her to follow you? Luckily, she followed you... How sweet! Well... In any case, it gives us hope for your family of so-called vampires which don't bite and don't drink human blood. At least, not like we do."

He was unhealthy, I'd already sensed it when he came before to the chateau, and when I'd overheard their conversation.

"I'm going to leave you, I've felt and seen what I had to see. My meal awaits me somewhere. Darren, let us know when you'll be back among your own kind. Don't bother, I know the way out!"

With this, he left the room. It had only lasted a few minutes, but it seemed an eternity. I didn't like those vampires.

"What exactly was he looking for, Darren?"

"I told you that we were of several kinds, and not all good ones. Alexandre isn't one of the good ones, as you were twice able to establish. For twenty-six years, we'd no longer transformed anyone in my family. This, the other vampires don't appreciate. For them, it's against their nature; like feeding ourselves with capsules instead of drinking human blood from the source, if I can say it that way."

"But it's your choice!"

"Exactly. We try to live in harmony with human beings: There is one earth and we have to all live here as best as possible. To attack humans as Alexandre and others do, represents a danger for us. It creates tensions. There are good vampires like us, and those of the likes of Alexandre, who isn't the worst. The further we go eastward, the more wild and inhuman they become. They rape women, transform children and abandon them half-dead or half-alive, depending on how we see it. They live like animals. You noticed how he looked at you? If Alexandre had transformed you, your life would have been much worse than the previous one."

"I see. After all, legends are based on something real."

"Of course. There are three species of vampire, Lilly, and then there are wizards and human beings. Coming back to vampires again, as I said; there are the abandoned, which fortunately represent a minority, because they're not organised. They learn on the job how to survive and receive no help from anyone. They were transformed, then left. The vampires who do that are of the same race as Alexandre: They don't respect life, they respect nothing in fact. They're just faithful to their family, and yet... Then there's us: The kind ones, if I may say so. Sometimes, we collect the abandoned to give them a better life, because they didn't choose their condition. And then, now there's you," he concluded.

"Me? How am I different?"

"You're a vampire because you searched for it and wanted it ardently. Of course, there were reasons for it, but you are and will remain for a long time the first one, even if the result is a perfect success. But enough small-talk... How about if we danced a bit before the end of the ball?"

"Yes, of course," I answered.

Without Alexandre's intervention, I'd maybe have taken years to learn all I'd just heard. To believe in vampires, to be a vampire, was one thing, but there were also wizards, which I'd discovered in Scotland. To humans; vampires and wizards were just fables or species which had vanished.

If they knew, there would be a relentless war. The human being kills what it's afraid of, but the vampire possesses one weapon which the human doesn't have: The power to transform, and thus to enlarge its troops. I would thus discourage a human from engaging in such a battle; lost beforehand in my opinion. Darren was right: Living together was the best solution.

"Are you with me?" He asked suddenly.

"Yes, I was thinking about what you were just saying."

"I know."

He wanted to appear sorry, but I didn't believe it for a single moment.

"You haven't the right to do that, Darren."

"All right. In any event, your reasoning is correct."

"Darren!"

I placed my head on his shoulder, smiling, and carried on dancing with him, savouring the moment.

The ball was going at full swing, the group were great, playing requests for the guests. At about 5 o'clock in the morning, the room finally began to empty. The problem with vampires is that, since they don't need to sleep, they stay up very late. Fortunately, some humans were there. It was they who started the move to leave. I ended up alone with Darren; for the first time I was apprehensive about this moment. This evening, too many things had been said silently.

The door closed on the last guest. Darren turned to me and came as close as possible.

"Your ball was a success," he said.

"I believe so, yes."

I looked him right in the eyes, my hands were sweating beneath my gloves.

He gently moved my hair away from my face and slowly stroked my cheek. I put my hand on his and closed my eyes. For the first time, I felt his lips settling on mine, so soft, so hot. Never had anybody kissed me like this, with such passion. He slowly drew away from my face and continued to touch my hair. There was so much sweetness and tenderness in his gesture...!

"Don't leave now, Lilly, there's nothing obliging you to go. Your appointment with the doctor is in nine days, and you start back at work the following month. Stay a little longer," he pleaded.

"Marie says that you've become vulnerable because of me. If I represent a danger for you, I should leave."

"Marie talks too much. I know what I'm doing, believe me. But it's true that I need you near to me. If you're far away, that risks being worse. Trust me again once more."

"You're aware the time must come soon. I have no choice, Darren. It was part of our agreement, you remember?"

"Yes, I haven't forgotten. Things didn't have to turn out this way, but it happened."

"I know. This thought is far from my mind too. But if you truly want me to, then okay, I'll stay a bit longer."

"I really want it."

He hugged me tightly, then accompanied me back me up to my bedroom. He stopped in the doorway and murmured:

"Good night, Lilly."

I opened my door to wish him a good night as well, when he caught hold of my hand and pulled me to him. His eyes had changed colour. He leaned towards me, and kissed me, this time with ardour, and disappeared. I stayed there, still under the shock of such a kiss.

I went to bed, my head full of stars. I revelled in total happiness.

13

I emerged from my slumber at around 8am. I did a tour of the chateau, but saw nobody, it was still early. And yet, the night had been long.

I was walking in the courtyard with my cup of milk, when I saw Darren's car, he hadn't put it away in the garage. I went to contemplate it: It was an attractive sports car. The keys were on the dashboard. I looked all around... I was still alone.

I went up to my room to fetch my handbag. There was something I had to get, but anyway, I would be back before he awoke. I listened closely: There was no activity in the chateau.

I did however leave a note in the kitchen, to warn him of my little escapade: I didn't want him to believe that in the end, I'd gone! I came back down and settled in behind the steering wheel. I looked around towards the chateau one last time, then discreetly left. I waited until I'd passed through the gates before I put my foot down.

I was leaving for only the first time since my transformation. It's true that I hadn't gone far, just to the nearby village where I'd noticed a jewellery shop. I was hoping it would be open, since this was a Sunday.

I'd never really thanked Darren for what he'd done for me. I wanted to find him a present so that he'd think of me when I was no longer there, in the chateau. He'd given me my life. I could never forget it, his venom was flowing inside me. I thought that some jewellery would be perfect. It was a tiny gift compared to his, but what could I do otherwise, without ever disappointing him?

I parked in the small village square. Some shops were open: A small hardware store, the bakery, as well as a minimarket - which were no use to me, even on a Sunday morning - and thank God; the jewellery shop.

I pushed open the door of the shop, hoping to find something appealing there. A girl was standing behind the counter, adjusting a bracelet for a customer. This gave me a bit of time to wander around and get some ideas for my present. It would have to be special.

I lingered in front of the bracelets, but nothing pleased me. The next display case was for watches. I knew that Darren owned one which was very beautiful, and probably very old. These didn't compare!

"Hello," said the shopkeeper, after accompanying the lady with the bracelet to the door.

"Hello, Miss."

"May I help you?"

"I hope so! I'd like to find a present for a dear friend."

"A man?"

"Yes, a man…"

This detail made me smile, since I could have answered "No, a vampire!" I laughed silently, imagining her face, if I'd have said it.

"We have some very attractive rings. Shall I show them to you?"

"Yes, please."

She went back behind the counter and opened a display case which I hadn't previously seen. It'd been hidden by the other customer. I joined her.

"Silver?" She asked.

"Absolutely not! He hates silver."

Despite having evolved, silver was still a poison for vampires. I specified my choice:

"More like white gold or platinum, if you have it!"

"Of course," she said, smiling.

She moved over towards another display case, I went over as well. There was everything here: From simple rings to rings ornamented with a gemstone. I didn't know that men wore gemstones... They were very beautiful. I smiled: She knew that I'd found what I was looking for.

My choice was a kind of old-looking white-golden signet ring, set with a ruby; it would remind him of the ball. It was neither too big nor too small. The ruby was placed in its centre, supported by two sculptured hands. The detailing was incredibly fine and beautiful. A true goldsmith's work.

"I'll draw up the certificate of authenticity and prepare a gift-wrapped parcel. I'll need a few minutes."

"Thank you."

At this precise moment, my mobile rang. I apologised and withdrew into the corner. I was surprised, because it hadn't rung for months. I didn't recognise the number which was displayed, nevertheless, I decided to answer.

"Hello?"

"Hello Lilly," said Darren.

"How do you have this number?"

"I still have the card which you gave me at the club. Where are you?"

His tone was cold.

"In the village, I had to get something. I left you a note on the kitchen table. Are you irritated about the car?"

"No, not about the car. Couldn't you have waited until I'd got up?"

"Not for what I had to do. I had to go alone, forgive me. Anyway, I'm finished. I'll be back in a few minutes."

"I'm waiting for you!"

He hung up straight away. Obviously, he wasn't happy.

"Here it is Miss," said the shopkeeper, handing me the little package.

I paid her and went over towards the car. I was annoyed by that phone call.

The return to the chateau only took eight minutes. I parked in front of the steps where Darren was waiting for me. He looked furious.

"Give me the car keys," he exclaimed.

"I left them inside."

I delicately put the little package away in my pocket. It was clearly not the moment I'd dreamed of to offer it to him, unless he was going to calm down.

He sat down on the steps, I joined him there. A long silence followed. These minutes seemed an eternity. Should I start the conversation? I tried to listen to his thoughts, but I heard nothing; he must be blocking me somehow or other.

"Why can't I read you?" I asked without diverting my look away from the car.

"Experience, Lilly; which you don't have, I must remind you."

I frowned and understood that he wasn't angry: He'd been afraid that something would happen to me. What could happen to me? I'd soon have to face the outside world. I ought to expose myself to others... And alone! My first experience had gone very well. So, there was no reason to be afraid. For my part, in any case.

"If I stay locked in here, how do you expect me to manage on my own?"

"I'm not preventing you from going out. Just that I have to know, because I must - at least in the beginning – watch over you. It's my role."

"I understand, but I wasn't far away."

"Far enough that I wouldn't be able to intervene in time, just in case."

About which dangers was he speaking?

"Seriously, what could happen to me?"

"Everything and nothing. I don't think you're completely ready yet. I'm speaking at the level of your reactions, of your handling of a transformation in case of an external event. What would you have done if something had triggered it?"

"I would've left as you told me to do. I remember everything you tell me, Darren. You could try to trust me a little more."

"I do trust you, more than you think, but I'm wary of others. Any small difficulty could make you change. Are you conscious of it, at least?"

"I believe that the best thing would be to test me in a hostile environment," I said, laughing.

"It's not a game, Lilly."

"I know, and I'm fine. Look at me... Nothing happened, I simply left to do some shopping."

I thought again about my reaction in front of the seller, but I refrained from telling him about it.

I stood up suddenly. He raised his eyes towards me. Then, I delicately handed him the box containing the ring and mumbled to him, smiling:

"This is for you…"

He got up in turn, quite surprised.

"I don't see why."

"Hush! Open it, please."

He silently did so. I tried to read his thoughts: In vain, once again. His look stayed riveted to the open box. At last, he took the ring out of its case.

"It's very beautiful, Lilly. Thank you, I'm very touched."

He slipped it on. I went up to him and took his hand in mine.

"I wanted to thank you for all that you… For all you've done for me. Never has a human acted as you've done. You're the most remarkable being I've ever met. I don't know if you realise what you've brought me, but it's much more than immortality: You gave me energy, the essence of life. This isn't anything much, but when I'm no longer here, it'll remind you of me. I don't want you to forget me."

Without taking his eyes off our hands, he said to me:

"We're bound for all eternity, Lilly, this present wasn't necessary. Even without this ring, my thoughts will always be with you. You're the most stubborn and tenacious human being I know. Without your perseverance, you wouldn't have gained my confidence."

He drew me to him and muttered:

"How could I forget you, Lilly?"

Then, he hugged me. We stayed like this for a few minutes. The atmosphere was charged with a palpable emotion. He moved away slightly. I could read this emotion on his face and in his eyes. Could vampires cry?

14

Ten o'clock on the dot. Darren was outside my door, I felt him. What did he want so early in the morning? To check whether I'm still here? He knocked gently.

"May I come in?"

"Of course!"

He came and sat on the edge of my bed, having drawn the curtains.

"Today, we'll go to your home. Not in Paris, but to your house."

"Why?"

"I've many reasons. Firstly, it's because I'd like to see where you live; next, the place must be missing you. How long has it been since you were last there?"

"In June, I believe."

"You see, it's about time... Get yourself ready, I'll wait for you downstairs."

He got up and left the bedroom. I took less time than I would have believed to prepare myself. The idea of going to my home filled me with joy.

Darren put the details into the sat-nav. We would need just over two hours to get there, it was further than I thought. I lived in a small town on the border of the Oise, a long way from everything; in the countryside, yet close to my work. That was the advantage of it.

I looked at my house from the car. The shutters were open, the cats probably outside; a day like any other.

"It feels bizarre to be here," I said, my eyes still fixed on my house.

"Let's go!" He said, opening my car door from his seat.

His contact, so close, reminded me of the day of the ball. I searched in my bag to find my keys. They were right there where I'd put them five months previously. Passing in front of the letter box, Darren asked me:

"Aren't you going to look?"

Definitely, vampires were curious.

"No, everything should be in the house. A friend's taking care of it in my absence."

"Did she know it would be for so long?"

"Yes of course."

Darren's behaviour amused me; he was looking all around! Not out of concern, but out of pure curiosity. He no longer knew where to put his eyes. He was like a child and, for once, it was me who was in my element.

I was about to put the key into the lock, when the door opened.

"Lilly! What a surprise! How happy I am to see you," shouted Sandrine, my lifelong friend.

Her embrace started to suffocate me. She released me at last. I introduced her to Darren, as a musician friend I'd met in a club, which wasn't false. I didn't like lying to Sandrine, she'd sense it immediately. She knew me so well, and for such a long time! Would it still be this way, now that I was no longer quite the same? I told her that we were just dropping in, and that I'd be back as expected in December.

"No problem, Lilly, as you well know," she answered.

"I can't ever thank you enough."

She hugged me for the second time in only a few minutes, then whispered to me:

"He's handsome, your musician."

"I know," I said to her with a smile.

I watched her go off into the distance, saying that she was soon going to harass me into telling her more. She turned around twice to wave. I adored this girl.

"We can go in now," I said to Darren.

"I'm impatient to see your universe," he said, prodding me in the back.

"You're going to be disappointed."

"Let me be the judge of that."

Inside the house, the smell of cats filled my nostrils. Not the unpleasant smell of the litter, but that of the animals, their hormones. It was something new.

"Are my cats going to sense a difference?"

"Certainly. The cat is a special animal. What's more, vampires aren't appreciated much by animals."

"Aren't they going to love me anymore?"

"I don't know. Come on, show me around!"

I made him discover the kitchen first of all. Of course, this room wasn't very appealing to a vampire, but he found it pleasant. Out of politeness, maybe. He was more interested in the corner snug of my living-room, dedicated to books. Nothing like his, because my collection amounted to novels, some biographies and my historic books about Ireland.

"Could I borrow some?" He asked seriously.

"Take what you want, Darren, make yourself at home, as I do in your chateau. If you mislay one, it doesn't matter; unlike yours, I'll find another one in the bookshop around the corner."

This comment made him smile. He was now looking at my photos, but was impressed by my collection of DVDs. Now that I thought about it, I hadn't seen a television in the chateau. He roared with laughter reading the titles of such films as: "Interview with a vampire", "Underworld"... In brief, a fine collection of vampires. I looked at him.

"Did you really think I didn't believe in you?"

"To be fascinated doesn't mean to believe, Lilly."

"You're right, I was always taken with vampire stories."

"Write yours, now. You told me: "Writing, sometimes it's a chance to make people dream." If we can call this a dream..."

"Are you speaking seriously?"

"Naturally. Your story appears like fiction and could make a very good subject for a film."

"You're teasing me, Darren. We ought to remain discreet, yet you'd want to make me a star?"

"At least you don't underestimate your abilities!" He said, roaring with laughter.

I approached him and feigned an attack, which he evaded with disconcerting ease. Then, he headed to the garden, but this one didn't impress him at all. My partitioned-off four hundred square metres seemed tiny to him, compared with his own, but he did admit that it was well-kept, and lingered there awhile.

"Come, I'll show you the first floor," I shouted down from the staircase.

"Wait, come and look!"

What had he discovered in my garden?

"What's going on?"

I could see him, holding one of my cats in his arms. I approached slowly.

"He's adopted you, we might say. He's called Tenshi. It means Angel or Snow in Japanese, I never remember which."

"It suits him very well. In general, cats are suspicious towards us. It's strange, he has very soft fur."

I stroked him too, Tenshi purred. At least, one of my cats had accepted my new condition for the time being, which put me in an even better mood.

I then made him come and see the first floor which didn't interest him very much. None of my other cats showed even the tips of their noses. I rummaged in my wardrobe, I needed an extra bag to bring my things in.

"Do you want a coffee, Lilly?"

"Ah… Yes, thanks. But wait, I'll take care of it, you don't know the coffee machine."

"Oh! I'll manage it," he shouted from the kitchen.

I rejoined him. He handed me my cup and proclaimed:

"Now, we'll go to your apartment, to sort out your things, clear it out and then hand back the keys."

"All right."

"Then we'll come back here, put everything indoors, and then you can fetch your car back."

I started to smile: Darren was taking things in hand with the aim of my forthcoming reintegration.

"I'll follow you throughout the journey, don't smile at your semi-freedom! Then, we'll go back to the chateau. Does this plan suit you?"

"Yes, it's very good."

"We'll still have a little time for perfecting your education."

It took all day to do what we'd planned. There were many kilometres between each point, and loads of traffic. I got the deposit back from my apartment without any problem, and realised that I'd had no expenses since I'd been living in the chateau. Life as a vampire was economical! In any case, for me and at the moment.

When I passed through the gates of the property, a strange feeling came over me. This was the first time I'd come here in my car, but certainly wouldn't be the last. I was planning on returning as often as possible.

15

I allowed myself a moment's respite. I no longer had the apartment, I'd got my car back and all my clothes were either at home or here. I didn't like being so widely dispersed and I admit that these last few months had been more than turbulent. I liked being closed in, the feeling of having walls around me, feeling secure.

My life had changed, I would never have believed that being on top physical form would prove to be so agreeable. For those who've always been that way, nothing is more hideous than falling ill. Seriously, I'd like to say. Me, I lived through quite the reverse; like a rebirth, emerging from the tunnel. I walked towards the light, I left death behind. What a paradox!

I no longer dreaded the future, at least not in the same way. The fact of knowing that except for an accident, I had eternity to catch up for lost time, brought me a much deserved serenity. The only dark areas were called "doctor" - I could foresee difficult moments - and "work", because I didn't know at all how my return would go. As discreetly as possible, I hoped.

The time of the real apprenticeship had come, not simply learning on the job like in Scotland, even if in the end, things there might have been no different.

I couldn't read the whole of the book about the gifts; the most I could do was to refer to it at the relevant moment. I couldn't take it away or make any copies. Therefore, I had to learn it. There were still a few days left.

Late in the afternoon, Darren came to look for me to go to Paris. This evening, they were performing as "guests" in another club. I'd find myself on unknown territory. He asked me to observe, to feel, to get involved with people and to listen. In brief; to put all my vampiric senses on the alert. Smiling, he added that I shouldn't let myself get hypnotised by the concert; the implication being: By him. It made me laugh because, if that hadn't occurred the first time, I wouldn't even be here. But I would try to follow his directives in all seriousness.

An hour after our departure, we were parked in front of the club. I'd say that we'd driven well. Before getting out of the car, Darren asked me:

"Do you remember what I told you to do?"

"Yes: To open my eyes, my ears, stay on the alert and sense the world around me. To especially not be enthralled by the band which is performing here this evening."

"I'm serious, Lilly."

"Me too, Darren. Tell me, are you stressed by the concert or because of me?"

"A bit of both, to tell the truth."

He gently stroked my cheek, then placed a delicate kiss on my mouth, the first one since the ball.

"I trust you Lilly."

"So, don't worry."

The stage door was on one side of the club. So I entered alone, ready to confront the real world.

Behind the heavy smoked-glass door, there were some steps to descend, covered in a carpet which in the half-light appeared to be red. At the foot of these, I passed through a large curtain of the same colour and found a little room which looked like a cloakroom. On the left was a counter. A woman gave me a smile: It would appear that I had to leave my coat. I did so, and slipped the ticket into the pocket of my jeans. Then I headed to the only door, which was facing me. This place was more like a fortress than a Jazz club and it occurred to me that if I had to flee, it would be difficult to do so in a hurry. There were so many obstacles! I looked at the alternatives, just in case.

I found myself in a large room, more like a cellar. The ceilings were low, with alcoves; it was very beautiful and certainly very old. A quick glance allowed me to distinguish the bar on the right, long and made of wood. Some men were sitting in front of glasses. Two barmaids were taking care of them. A young girl was standing in front of me, an usherette. She showed me to a table near a wall. A small lamp hung over this one, the only detail which would've been able to bring a bit of charm to the place. It was rustic, uncomfortable and quite surprising for a Jazz club. In my opinion, they ought to invest in it a little, they would gain in terms of clientele. This place was wasted, considering the architecture.

"What can I bring you?" She asked in a monotone.

"A Corona," I answered in the same tone.

She turned her heels without a word. I sensed no unknown vampires in the place. I had another quick glance around the cellar, hoping to see something even a little pleasant. In the end, I understood the attitude of the waitress: It must be dull to work here. It was depressing and lifeless. I suddenly realised that there wasn't even any background music. I could just hear the noises coming from the stage, closed off by a curtain. The room was empty. This situation made me feel uneasy for the group.

She came back with my Corona, garnished with a slice of lemon, put it down on a coaster and left again without saying a word. I had noticed one thing: I couldn't manage to enter into the minds of the humans. Maybe due to my lack of experience? Or because they weren't worth the effort?

I began to quietly sip my beer and a couple settled themselves down not far from me, when I heard a noise resounding in my head. A group of about ten people had just made their entrance. All were vampires. All were unknown to me, I could only hear their voices in a hubbub. An icy breeze accompanied them when they walked past me. I lowered my head to make myself discreet, which served no purpose. I heard them. Probably they'd also sensed my presence.

Seeing the smile from the waitress, I got the impression that they were regular customers. As the minutes went by, the room filled up. Everything was happening quickly now. We'd arrived early. For Darren, this was normal; for me, it had after all allowed me to get my bearings.

They dimmed the lights, which brought a different aspect to the room. The curtains were opened by hand, by a man. This detail truly went along with all the rest of it: Old-fashioned! There was much to be done here.

At last I saw Darren again and got to hear this evening's group. The man presented the musicians; applause came from all around. Darren adjusted the microphone in front of him, discreetly bid us good evening and began the first song.

I was reminded of the evening of the ball, when he sang for me. He wasn't a singer, but it was something he could incorporate into their show. Of course, the Jazz they played hardly lent itself to it, but it would change the feel. I stored this suggestion away in a corner of my mind to tell him later on. I liked what the group were doing. It was different to what I generally listened to, but this music had the ability to relax me.

The group of vampires gave things a bit of atmosphere, which amazed me because we ought to remain discreet. I was more on my guard than ever. Something about them disturbed me, without being able to say what. In the break, Darren came to join me and ordered a cocktail.

"Have you played here before, Darren?"

"No, this is the first time. The boss is a friend of Vic's, that's why we accepted. I don't like performing very much, except at the club."

"I understand you, it's different. Very much so, even!"

"Don't you like this place?"

"Not much. They don't look after it at all, and also, the people aren't very pleasant. It's really nothing like it is in your club."

"Yes, our clientele are mainly friends. That changes everything."

"Sometimes enemies as well…"

I remembered the fire they'd had, even though I hadn't been present.

He looked around discreetly, finishing his glass. He put it on the table, kissed me, smiled, and returned to settle himself back down on the stage. The other group members had already gone back to their places.

The concert was going very well, people were appreciating their music, when four individuals came into the room. They were oddly dressed, all in black, with boots and long coats. They reminded me of vigilantes, they immediately aroused in me a strange feeling, like suspicion. They took seats at a table to my right, but somewhat far off. We were separated by the group of vampires. The men didn't appear to have come here for the music.

Suddenly I heard Darren's voice resounding in my head. Instinctively, I turned to him.

"Pay careful attention, Lilly, they're hunters!"

"Hunters?"

I told myself that my impression had been well-founded.

"Yes, of vampires."

"How could they know what we are?"

"They aren't here for us, but for the group sitting near you. And to answer your question, they've no way of knowing about it for themselves, they've been informed!"

"But who…?"

"Anybody. One day, you said that man eradicated what he feared. Now, you know that some of them do know and want to exterminate us."

"My God!"

"Yes, and often in his name, besides! But they aren't here for us, remain cautious. They can't know who you are."

"What's going to happen?"

"I don't know that. Not yet."

"Can you read them?"

"Yes. (He paused a moment) fortunately!"

"Who denounced them?"

"The waitress."

I turned my head to her. I saw her differently now, and understood why she'd smiled when they'd arrived.

"Did you know when we came here, that this could happen?"

"It can happen anywhere. But no, I wouldn't have exposed you to such a danger. Stay on your guard, in any case."

"Yes, Darren, but how?"

I asked myself the same question: What could I do, just in case? How was I to react, facing such a danger? What ought my attitude to be?

"Don't lose sight of them... The humans, I mean to say."

"Why not warn the vampires?"

"I'm trying to get in touch with them, but I don't know them. Therefore I can't speak to them as I do with you."

"And if I...?" I began to say

"No!"

This word resounded in my head.

"You, don't you budge, whatever happens," he continued calmly.

I could've sworn that his shout in my head had also coincided with the sound of the saxophone. That note had seemed louder than the rest.

"Okay. I Promise, Darren."

"Very good, Lilly. Very good."

I therefore observed the slightest of their movements. I was on the defensive, but allowed nothing to show. I pretended to listen to the concert like everybody else or almost everybody, in the room.

Suddenly I felt my nails metamorphosing and I concentrated immediately on an object, which resulted in an instant retraction. I was rather proud of this control. Nobody noticed it, I was grateful for the low light.

I saw the waitress taking her place behind the bar, the time for kindness had just come to an end. One of the men got up and went to join her. I didn't hear what they said, they were too far away. On the other hand, I clearly saw her pointing out the table of vampires. I didn't understand how they couldn't sense the danger surrounding them, since I'd been capable of doing so. Maybe they were feigning it? They were talking, drinking as if nothing was amiss.

"Why don't they react?" I asked finally.

"I don't know. It's really strange, indeed. They don't seem to be on the alert, they aren't cautious."

The man sat down without taking his eyes off them. Four against ten; logically, we had to win. But was anything logical here?

It was one of the first nights I'd spent out in the world and I tried to remember whether, before all of this, there'd been things in my life which I could link to vampires or wizards, now that I knew of the existence of other "species". They seemed to be all around, but if I looked at the people here in the room, I could say that most of them here were fringe elements; none more so than the four men dressed in black, after all. They looked like a gang of youths on a night out.

My gaze went from the bar to their table, by way of the stage. Nothing was happening. The hunters were certainly waiting for the end of the concert. I supposed that they had to remain discreet. In any case, I didn't imagine they'd launch a vendetta inside this club, at the risk of standing out and so exposing to the world the existence of monsters. A general panic would inexorably follow.

The concert came to an end at its set time, and still nothing had happened. Darren came back to join me. I got up, thinking that we were going to leave, but he signalled to me to sit back down again. I looked inquisitively at him. He bent over towards me and murmured:

"I'm going to collect our fee, then we can leave. Stay here."

He headed over to one of the barmen, at the bar. This one handed him an envelope which he slipped into his pocket. It was at this precise moment that the men decided to act. They leapt up and took double-barrelled rifles out from their long coats, which they hadn't removed. They trained guns on us, they yelled at us to be quiet. I don't know why, but they made some people leave. Then, they went over to the group.

I stayed sitting in my place to observe the spectacle. Darren was across the room, still stuck in the bar. I looked at him and tried to communicate with him, but he remained mute. He was probably gauging the situation. Myself, I looked all around to find an escape route. The stage appeared to be a good option. The four men were surrounding the table, still keeping the vampires under watch. They seemed to have been brought out of their lethargy now, as if they hadn't noticed the presence of the predators before. It was strange. A man spoke and addressed the vampires:

"Don't try anything, remain seated for the moment."

Then, addressing the few people still left in the club:

"You; remain quiet and nothing will happen to you!"

One of the customers tried a rash move, hoping to disarm one of the men. He found himself on the ground straight away, a barrel of a rifle pinned to his temple.

"I told you not to move!" Yelled one of the aggressors.

He crouched on the floor and made himself more unobtrusive than ever.

The predator went back to join the others and everything happened very quickly. They began by aiming blows to the head of one of the vampires, the one who seemed the youngest in human terms. He was fair-haired, not very tall, and very slim. He was thrown over to my table which overturned, so serving as a shield for me. I could only see the top of his body. The man rushed over onto him and forced a stake into his heart, which instantly paralysed him. The memory of the cocoon came back to me, where Albert had been imprisoned in Scotland. He too, had received a stake in his heart.

The vampire's head was turned towards me, his eyes expressed an immense terror. I couldn't look at anything else, being hypnotized by his gaze. What could I do?

Darren still remained silent. I bent over to one side a little to look at the rest of the room, but what I saw was unreal: The room was empty, with the exception of the man still sitting on the vampire, the wounded vampire, and myself.

I began to panic, then an idea came into my mind: What if I finally helped the vampire? The two of us against this man, it could be done, right? Even if we were both very young.

I tried desperately to get in touch with the vampire, when one of the men rushed back into the room. I wisely sat back down again behind my table.

"So?" He said, approaching.

The man sitting on the vampire got up and took a position in front of his victim's head, I could see him perfectly. I backed away towards the wall. With a discreet signal, he advised me to remain quiet. I huddled myself up a bit more to show him that I'd understood. This wasn't the moment to play the heroine.

"Go on, finish him off," shouted the last one to arrive. "This evening, it's your baptism, right?"

"Yes," answered the other one, still looking at me, as if to apologise for what I was witnessing.

He took a phial from his parka and sprinkled it on the vampire, who still couldn't move. A strong smell of petrol filled the room. I understood at this moment what he was preparing to do. It was the only means to exterminate a vampire: Fire. Then he brought out a box of matches and squatted near to the vampire. I watched the scene with terror, powerless facing this spectacle. I wasn't even capable of coming to the aid of one of my own kind! I felt tears running down my cheeks. He lifted his head by his hair and murmured to him:

"You are an error of nature, friend. You're going to die by my hands. Then, we'll take care of your friends."

He spat in his face.

I began to realise what Darren had told me: Fear brings violence. The human was afraid, he acted out of treachery. The man stepped back a few paces and struck his match. He was looking at the flame, he seemed to be mad. Then, he casually threw it onto the powerless vampire. His body immediately caught fire, I heard his scream, piercing and high-pitched. I tried to block my ears, it was unbearable!

I couldn't take my eyes off him, his body shrivelled up at an outrageous speed; like paper. The smell was horrible. The combustion lasted barely a few minutes. I could still make out his features, but only as a sculpture of grey sand.

The man approached it, quite proudly, and gave it a kick. The shape disintegrated straight away. I remained hypnotised, incapable of even the slightest movement.

The man came over and drew level with me. My first reflex was to press myself even harder to the wall, like a cornered animal, but he offered me a friendly hand. I grabbed it, he slowly helped me up. Was it my turn? He drew me roughly to him, fixed me in his gaze and said:

"You saw nothing, heard nothing. It wasn't anything very important: This man was sick and we did him a service by freeing him. Have you got that?"

"Yes Sir."

I had nothing else to say to him. Without doubt, this man was an idiot. It was better to agree with him wholeheartedly. With a finger, he pointed to the stage.

"That way! Let's avoid anyone seeing you."

I started walking faster and faster and disappeared into the corridors of the club, in search of the exit and of Darren. I opened a door which brought me onto the pavement, right in front of the car. Darren got out and came running towards me. He held me tightly in his arms. At last I could let go of my sadness. He carried me to my seat without a word.

The return journey was done quickly. Darren informed me that all the vampires in the group had been exterminated. He still wondered why none of them had reacted, or even sensed the danger. I remained prostate in my silence, I had no answer to give him. We were, for our part, safe and sound.

That I found myself trapped in that room was the fruit of a combination of circumstances. By falling over, the table had hidden me from everybody's sight. They made the potential witnesses leave in order to successfully complete their task of de-vampirisation. They didn't suspect that they had another of their prey right under their noses.

From this day forward, my view of humans would be totally different and merciless. The image of this killing would remain engraved in my memory for centuries to come.

16

I walked along the white and blue corridors. I remember previously, that I used the blue lines drawn on the floor, as a route to follow.

I ended up in the reception area and found a place to sit, out of the way a little. Cubicle B, reserved for doctor Moonroe, was almost full, but that area had only seven chairs. Facing me, there were two men, one much younger than the other. Perhaps father and son, but Italians as far as I could tell. Two seats separated me from a woman who was absorbed with her magazine. She hadn't even looked up when I came in. Since the men had arrived after me, I could conclude that one sole person was ahead of me. It was just past noon; the doctor was late, as he often was.

In spite of the exorbitant price of the care, loads of people passed in front of our cubicle. Of all nationalities, sizes and classes. But then health is priceless...

It was easy to tell the patients from the employees here. I'm not talking about doctors or nursing staff, who wore uniforms, but about those wearing a badge.

This was the first time I'd felt so well in such places, I even had the feeling that I didn't need to be here. The transformation had been beneficial, I was doing marvellously. The only fly in the ointment, was maybe this need for regeneration. Martin still hadn't said anything to me.

I would have to be careful with the doctor. Tell him the minimum. But knowing him, he'd ask a million questions.

He opened the door and invited me in.

"But it looks like you're well!" He said directly.

"Yes, indeed so, doctor."

He read his notes to remind himself of the previous problems which I'd presented him with.

"Well, let's start again. Regarding the numbness in your right hand, do you still have this sensation?"

"No, it's really calmed down."

"All right, let's talk about your dizziness. Still as frequent in the morning or when you feel very tired?"

He raised his head from his notes and waited for my answer.

"No, I'm no longer dizzy. I just had a cold, a few days ago."

"Your headaches?"

"Also finished," I said, smiling.

Ought I to invent something to appear more credible and avoid his suspicions?

"Well, tell me what's not okay, then!"

"Honestly, everything's all right."

"And in your opinion, how is it that, all of a sudden, everything's all right?" He asked with a note of suspicion.

"It is not all that sudden, I've felt it gradually. This summer, I took my holidays by the sea, and I'm still on sabbatical leave for a few days yet. I think they're two important factors. I feel truly better. My pains have disappeared."

"So, the rest and the peace did you good... Perfect! Are you continuing to take your medicine?"

This was the tricky question I hadn't wanted him to ask. I'd be obliged to lie.

"Yes, of course. Do you believe that I could reduce them, even stop them if my condition stays like this?"

"Some yes, others no. Some you'll have to take for the rest of your life," he stated.

"All right."

"Well, let's go to the next room, I'm going to examine you."

I was becoming more and more anxious. I undressed as I would normally do, and lay down on the examination table. For the first time in my life, I did it with neither pain nor grimace. He noticed it, naturally.

"Oh! Yes, I can see that you've got much better. I'm very happy for you and I sincerely hope that it continues in this way. It seems that you're finding some balance. Are you eating new things?"

"A lot of fruit and vegetables, some meat twice a week. You know that I don't like meat, but I force myself, to bring me protein. Lots of fruit juice, plus long forest walks. The success of my physical form is a mixture of all this. Furthermore, I go to bed early, I sleep for at least eight hours. And believe me, I feel so good that I wouldn't change any of the new rules I've adopted in my life."

"You're perfectly right. The colour of your skin has changed… I think you didn't take enough advantage of the sun this summer."

"No, with my allergies, I avoid exposing myself for too long."

I was happy about this allergy: It allowed me to justify my paleness.

He took my hand and looked at the veins on the back of it, frowning.

"Is there a problem, doctor?"

"I don't believe so, but the tone of your skin gives your veins a strange colour. I'm going to prescribe you a blood test, perhaps it'll be necessary to change the dosage of your blood-thinner."

"All right," I said, forcing myself to smile.

"Let's look at your reflexes."

He proceeded with my examination as he'd always done: Tapping my knees or the sides of my ankles, possibly my elbows. My reflexes were good, but I'd already recovered my reflexes a few months after my stroke.

The examination ended with a series of balance tests, which I normally failed. I passed them successfully. I tried hard to feign some failures, but he wasn't fooled. I got dressed again silently, I heard him scribbling on my file.

"I'm surprised by so many positive points. The blood tests will maybe help me to understand better. Have you told me everything, Lilly?"

"Yes, what do you think I'm hiding from you?" I shouted from the next room where I still lingered.

"I don't know. I've looked after you for such a long time… I admit that this is the first time I've found you in such good shape. Thus, I'm asking myself…"

"Is it so exceptional?"

"A complete recovery after a stroke is possible, especially at your age. It's actually the stroke which wasn't normal, but I can't see how it would take care of your other illnesses. They're real, diagnosed and undergoing treatment. I've never heard of a complete cure for certain ones; it would be a first!"

"I don't know, I'm not a doctor. I just tell you what I feel. You know, I've stopped listening to my body. Maybe this is a reason."

"Why didn't it happen before, in that case?"

"Because before the stroke, I'd never nearly died. Things were different."

"Very true."

When I came back to my seat in front of him, he was looking concerned.

"I don't understand you, you should be happy with how I am!"

"I am... It's just that I'm a scientist and I need to understand. If we can find a treatment thanks to my research on a patient who's been cured, imagine...!"

I sensed trouble heading this way. Of course this man was so brilliant that he wouldn't drop this so readily! I respected him for his tenacity, I wasn't going to hate him for the same reason.

"There's nothing to research: I got better, that's all. And I think my mind did a lot of it."

"Go and tell a sick person with a terminal illness, that to think more positively would help him to recover: He'd laugh in your face, Lilly!"

"That's not what I'm saying, I'm talking about my case. I don't have cancer, me; I don't have a terminal illness."

"No, but you were so ill! This recovery seems like a miracle. Well, while we wait for the results of the further examinations which I'm prescribing you, let's be happy with this state of affairs. Have the blood test and see my secretary as usual for the MRI and the scintigraphy."

"Why so many things?"

"I told you: I like to understand."

"Okay."

I left the office and succeeded in arranging all my appointments during the following week. Everything must be done before I went back to work, I couldn't allow myself to be absent yet again. I stopped at the blood analysis laboratory, at the end of the corridor. It was quick; for once, there was only me there.

I joined Darren, who was waiting for me in the car-park. He didn't like hospitals.

"How did it go?" He asked straight away.

"Not very well I'm afraid: He spoke of a miracle, and made me do a series of examinations. He already sees himself with the Nobel Prize. My God, how stupid doctors are! If we're sick, that's no good; if we're no longer so, that's not normal either. I do apologise, but I sense trouble stacking up."

He put his hand on my arm.

"We're going to get by, don't worry."

"Maybe Martin could talk to him? To try to convince him to forget about it?"

"I don't know whether they know each other, but it's true that between colleagues, he could contact him without arousing suspicion. Very good idea! Let's go back home, now."

I passed the time on the return journey by looking outside. I thought of what I'd just been through and about what was going to happen in the days to come. My final days off wouldn't be as serene as I'd been hoping for.

"I'm going to convene a restricted council: Martin, Marie, Vic, you and me. We're calmly going to discuss the situation," exclaimed Darren.

Obviously, this was bothering him too.

"I agree. I'm afraid of being put in the limelight. This doctor is highly esteemed, it's not for nothing that I chose and kept him. But I know I won't be able to reason with him. If, for him, my cure looks like a miracle, he'll want to talk about it. To attract new grants for his work, for example. He can't let it silently pass him by. It's too important, you understand? In the worst case, I'll have to disappear."

"It's out of the question, Lilly: You're staying here. You have your life, your friends, your work. Running away is out of the question. We're going to find a solution, don't you worry."

"That's easy to say!"

I felt tears flowing down my cheeks. When I arrived at the chateau, I went to take refuge in my bedroom. As for Darren, he convened the council.

A good hour later, he knocked on my door. I was standing at the window contemplating the park. There was no sign of the storm of the previous few days.

Darren came over to me and wrapped his arms around me. Since the ball, this was his second gesture of physical affection. I closed my eyes to savour this short moment's peace of mind before the likely storm.

"They're here, Lilly. Are you coming?"

I didn't answer, but turned towards him, still in his arms. Our gazes met one another's, I lost myself in his. He slowly bent over towards me, placed a kiss on my lips and whispered to me:

"We're going to pull through, stop worrying."

By way of an answer, I held his face in my hands this time, to kiss him as I'd wanted to do for such a long time. Our embrace lasted for several minutes, a pure fusion of shared yet not completely revealed love. He gently took my hand and led me towards the door.

"They're waiting for us," he repeated, as if to apologise for cutting this moment short.

"I know."

They were sitting near the fire, in the same place where we so often had our breakfast. Martin and Marie were in the armchairs, Vic was contemplating the flames, leaning on the fireplace. Upon our entrance, Martin stood up to let me have his place. Darren spoke.

"You're not unaware that Lilly saw her doctor today. To put it simply, let's say that he finds her recovery to be miraculous, and therefore, he wants to carry out more detailed examinations on her, with a view to saving other people."

"I always thought that what you did was madness, Darren!" Marie intervened. "Dangerous for our community, for you, and now for her."

"I should remind you that without "HER", your dear friend would still be stuck in his cocoon. Have a bit of respect, Marie; you're talking about Lilly. She's one of us now, and we should stick together to solve this problem."

"Let's eliminate the doctor!" She said calmly.

"Marie, if you carry on like this, I'm going to exclude you from the discussion."

"I'm only offering ideas, Darren!"

"What examinations did he ask for, Lilly?" Martin asked, to put an end to their quarrel.

"A blood test, an MRI and a scintigraphy."

Martin looked around us, his hand on his chin, with a pensive face.

"We're not at risk of being unmasked with the MRI and the scintigraphy. Have you already done the blood test?"

"Yes, I always do it there."

"Vic, you're going to go and swap Lilly's blood for this one."

Martin handed him a phial; it contained my infected blood from a few days ago. Vic carefully slipped it into his pocket.

"Go... And don't draw attention to yourself, Vic," he added, to hurry him along.

"Don't worry!"

"That phial contains your blood which was infected with your flu. It reduces your vampire characteristics, but we'll only gain a little time, because I analysed it and found no trace of your human illnesses there. Your doctor is very ambitious, if I may say so. He'll do anything to get his medical discovery. Essentially, he won't drop the matter just like that. When do you see him again?"

"He should call me in a few days, I suppose. Why did I catch the flu, though?"

"We'll talk about that again later. We'll tackle one problem at a time, shall we?"

"Yes, of course."

I looked at Darren, maybe I'd find an answer in his eyes... But he was looking at the fire in a preoccupied way. Was he regretting my therapeutic transformation, now that things were taking a dangerous turn? Did he think he'd made a mistake, as Marie would so often suggest?

We remained there searching for a solution, and especially to wait for Vic's return. A few hours later, he eventually reappeared and handed my blood sample to Martin, who immediately put it away in his case.

"How did it go? You took a long time!" Darren exclaimed with an impatient tone.

"There was nobody there... The advantage with private clinics! It took a long time, yes, but the journey also took me a while, Darren. I proceeded to swap the blood and the labels over, all without leaving any evidence. This mission was delicate, so I had to take my time. The next time..."

"Thank you Vic," I said suddenly.

I got up straight away to give him a kiss on the cheek and squeeze his arm. He needed to calm down.

"You're welcome, Lilly," he answered, all the way down from his great height of six foot four. "We're a family and you're the latest to join us, we should take care of you."

I returned his smile.

"Well, we can go and rest now" announced Martin. "Tomorrow, I'll call Moonroe, I'll come up with a good excuse to meet him. I'll tell him that I've known you for a long time. I am your family doctor, in a way."

"Very well," agreed Darren. "We'll await your news."

"If he calls me in the meantime, I'll let you know," I added.

Everybody left for their homes. Darren and I, we ended up alone in the corner by the fire, which we contemplated silently.

My mind couldn't help but to run in all directions. At this precise moment, I would like to have known the future, and I hoped that we wouldn't end up with Marie's solution. This doctor had helped me throughout the whole of my human life, I didn't want to imagine that we would do him any harm, particularly because of me. Maybe the act of bringing him into the family would tidy matters up? He would then understand the need to conceal his discovery, which in fact, wasn't one at all.

"Maybe that's a solution, indeed," Darren said suddenly, listening to me once again.

"I don't want this man to die on my behalf. He's done so much for me, you know."

For once, I didn't reproach him for his intrusion into my thoughts.

"I know," he said, getting up.

He went to a large, ancient piece of furniture and opened its doors. A piano appeared; another one.

"Come here beside me," he said, settling himself down there.

I sat down by his side and put my head on his shoulder.

"What do you want me to play?"

"Whatever you want, I'm exhausted. Something soft."

He turned to me, smiling, then he took my hand, which he put on his leg. He kissed my forehead, I returned his smile and lost my gaze in his for a short moment. He began playing a soft melody which was unknown to me. Enchanting. It made me open my eyes again, I watched his fingers going along the keyboard.

"Who is this piece by?"

"By me."

I rested my head against him, savouring this moment which seemed to me timeless. The music, along with the crackling of the fire, led me to forget all of my problems. This contact, so close to Darren, was reassuring.

"I wrote this melody after seeing you for the first time at the club."

"Did you give it a title?"

"Yes: "Carefree"."

He finished playing and put his arm around my shoulder. Only the noise of the fire crackled in the room. The melody, it was still in my head.

"I didn't think that Professor Moonroe would react like that. If I'd known, I wouldn't have gone to this appointment. After all, nothing obliged me to go there."

"Don't you believe that it would have seemed odd for you to miss an appointment after so many years? And even so, it would only postpone the problem, Lilly. We're now going to face up to it, in order to be at peace. Vic did what was necessary, let's wait and see. We'll decide what to do, when the time comes."

"Yes, okay."

His voice was calm and peaceful. I liked the tranquillity, the strength and the serenity which this man exuded. He made me feel secure.

"Would you accompany me to the next appointment, Darren?"

"And…?"

"I don't know… Wouldn't you have some dissuasive power to help him not to dig too much into my state?"

"All vampires have this power, but before using it, let's see the way things are going."

"Do I have it too?"

"Yes, but you're too young to make use of it. It takes years for it to be effective. I'm sorry..."

He slowly placed himself astride the stool and looked at me. I did the same. We were face to face.

He took hold of my legs, crossed them over his and pulled me towards him.

"What are you doing?"

"What we both desire, Lilly. Am I wrong?"

I didn't answer. He put both his hands at the bottom of my back. They seemed to have become so hot... Then, he began covering my face with kisses. I closed my eyes.

"You'd hidden this shyness from me," he whispered.

"Certain things need to be discovered..."

"You're right."

"Are you disappointed?"

"No, on the contrary."

He resumed his kisses and, for the second time today, our lips found one another's. But this time, it was different: Our closeness made me feel his hands and lips more intensely. He felt it too; but him, he knew how to manage this kind of situation. I gently pushed him away and showed him my nails. He smiled and put my hands on his legs. Then, he bent over towards me again, opened his mouth and showed me his canines. While I was frowning, he said to me:

"It's a normal reaction, you don't have to be afraid of it. Not here, not with me, Lilly. Attraction... Remember," he said softly.

I ran my hands over his face, staring attentively at his eyes which had become blue. His mouth, while deadly, was nevertheless so attractive... I hadn't felt his teeth while kissing him. Then I stroked his neck and came to the knot which tied his hair. Tenderly, I let it fall loosely. Once again I took hold of his face and kissed it.

My heart was aflame, I could feel the blood running in my veins, I surrendered to my senses, my body liberated itself. I'd become a vampire and I intended to live it to the full.

17

The telephone rang at eight o'clock and brought me out of my half-sleep.

"Hello Lilly."

"Hello doctor, what's going on?"

I didn't think I'd be receiving this phone call so soon, which immediately made me feel uneasy.

"I received the results from your examinations."

"Already? Is there a problem?"

"I would say that the problem is, that there isn't one."

I remained speechless. I didn't know what to say.

"It's a total remission, even a cure. I can't understand it. A diet or a different lifestyle wouldn't cure certain pathologies, except in your case, it would appear. Or perhaps you're not telling me everything. I also searched for traces of your medicine in your blood: There were none!"

"It's probably a mistake in the laboratory..."

"I doubt it. Would you agree to submit yourself to another series of examinations, just in case there really has been an error? Your appointment for your MRI is at 11am, I believe. Shall we see you at 2pm?"

"All right, but promise me one thing."

"Yes, tell me."

"I don't want to become a guinea pig. If I'm cured, so much the better. I very much deserve it, after all I've endured!"

"It's a promise, but if that's the case, if you really are cured, I need to understand why. Other sick people deserve what's happened to you today. You can understand that, right?"

"Of course, but let's wait for these new tests before claiming victory. Maybe it's just a remission, it wouldn't be the first time."

"Indeed. See you later, Lilly."

He hung up. I stayed there, thinking.

I took a shower to relax and dressed myself warmly. The temperature outside was getting lower and lower; winter had set in for sure. I wasn't afraid of the cold, on the contrary, but I had to pay attention to this kind of detail which could draw the attention of common people, and even more so the doctor.

I found Darren and Hector in the kitchen, as with every day at this hour. My coffee had already been served. I approached Darren, a little bit hesitant because of our intimacy last night. He turned to me, a big smile lit up his face. He gently took hold of my hand, drew me towards him and placed a kiss on my cheek, whispering me a hello. I answered with a smile. My heart was pounding. I took a seat where my coffee was. Hector looked at us in amusement.

"I received a call from Moonroe: I have to see him again in the afternoon. That works out well, because my MRI takes place today too."

"Did he say anything in particular?"

"The results are very good, too good; he wants to redo the test. I suggested to him that it could be an error in the laboratory. I deduced that he hadn't spotted my flu either. At least, he didn't say anything about it."

"What time is the appointment?"

"2pm. Can you come along with me?"

"Of course," he said, caressing my hand to reassure me.

For the first time I heard the intercom for the gate. Hector had left the kitchen, so it was Darren who answered the videophone. This place would never cease to surprise me. Almost everything had been preserved within its proper period, but all these things concealed a little marvel of technology. He hung up and looked at me.

"Will you come with me? We have a delivery of wood."

I looked at him, rather surprised. He came over to me.

"Some wood for the fireplaces... Because I'm a romantic."

"I'll come along with you, but don't count on me to bring it in!" I said in all seriousness.

"No, that's Hector's role. Us, we'll just sign for it" he stated with a wink.

"You're a snob!"

"No, just an old man."

I burst into a loud laugh, he always took me by surprise. Then, I accompanied him up to the gate where an enormous lorry was waiting. He showed the man where to unload the wood and signed the receipt.

It was time to go to my appointments at the hospital. Darren called Martin and gave him the information that we had. Martin promised to join us. He wanted to attend my appointment, which reassured me. One hour later, we were ready to face the professor.

I went to my MRI and to my scintigraphy. Just as Martin had said, these two examinations presented no danger. We were waiting in the waiting room. As usual, the professor was late. I sensed that Darren felt uneasy. I took his hand, hoping that this gesture would reassure him, and suggested that he wait for us in the car. I had no idea why he didn't like hospitals. Martin, he was reading a medical magazine.

Finally, the professor called me. He was surprised to see that I wasn't alone. On passing through the doorway, Martin introduced himself: Moonroe answered him politely, and nothing more. He certainly didn't want to see his name linked with that of a stranger.

Moonroe sat down behind his desk, invited us to sit down, then opened my medical records.

"I have the results of your last examinations."

He opened two big envelopes and held the images up in front of the window.

"Everything seems normal," he asserted.

He raised his head and looked at me.

"You appear to be in great shape," he said.

My generally excellent state was bothering him. Martin decided to intervene.

"Professor Moonroe, allow me…"

"Please go ahead, dear colleague," he answered reluctantly.

"Lilly is ill and this has been the case since birth. I say this with full knowledge of the facts: I've looked after of her for quite a few years as a friend of the family. What's more, it was me who advised her to consult you. This isn't the first time she's got better, you must admit."

"But this is the first time her results have been not only this good, but also this physically visible," argued Moonroe.

"I concur, but we should be delighted with it. Lilly told me that you could find no trace of her medicine in your analysis?"

At this point, he handed him a sheet of paper which Moonroe examined with interest.

"Here are Lilly's last results. They date from a few days ago, when she contracted the flu. Believe me, without medication, they wouldn't be this good."

"Why give her a blood test for a simple case of flu?"

"You know her... We're always wary with our girl Lilly! I just preferred to make sure that it wasn't something else."

"I'm going to redo her complete blood report. I don't doubt the competence of our laboratory, but if a mistake was made there, I ought to worry about it. It harms the reputation of the clinic. Excuse me for a moment, please."

He got up and left the room. I turned to Martin.

"Where's he going?"

"I don't know, this man is stubborn!"

Martin rummaged in his case, brought out some tablets, and handed them to me.

"Take your medicine, Lilly. If it's the only thing that's troubling him at the moment, let's make this obsession go out of his head."

"But... Isn't it dangerous?"

"Don't worry, I'm here."

"Okay..."

I swallowed my three daily tablets.

Moonroe returned, armed with a hypodermic needle, a tourniquet and some test tubes. He went into the next room and invited me to join him.

"Sit down here, I'm going to do this blood test myself," he said.

"Don't you trust my doctor?" I asked, rolling up my sleeve.

"Of course, yes!"

Then, he raised his head towards me and whispered:

"You feel perfectly well, don't you? In that case, why have you brought him along? Don't you have more confidence in me?"

He pushed the needle into my arm. I didn't flinch.

"Yes, I do feel very well," I answered, watching my blood flowing into the first tube.

Strangely, to see my blood made me freeze. I raised my eyes and my gaze was drawn to his neck. A strange idea crossed my mind and straight away I tried to take my eyes off his flesh beneath which his life-blood flowed. His life so fragile at this moment. Then, suddenly, I heard the test tubes fall on the floor, which brought me out of my stupor. Moonroe's face had an expression of horror. The next instant, the professor collapsed on the floor.

I noticed that Martin was in the room. I stared at him, trying to understand.

"He... He died?" I asked.

"No, but I had to neutralise him: You were transforming yourself without being aware of it, and he watched you doing it."

Martin picked up the phials of blood, which he put on the table. Then, he bent over Moonroe, proceeded to do a quick examination, and opened the door of the office. Finally, he called the secretary.

"Miss, please! Your boss has had a stroke!"

He looked at me and told me not to move. The secretary ran in, then phoned the casualty department.

Martin had laid the professor on his side so that he wouldn't suffocate. A few moments later, the emergency doctors took him away. They confirmed that he'd had a stroke, but the man was out of danger. On exiting the hospital, Martin informed Darren about what had happened. The latter came over to me.

"Do you understand, now, why I don't consider you completely ready to face this world yet?" He said to me.

"But I didn't do anything!"

"You did nothing because Martin prevented you: It was the last thing we would have wanted, for you to jump on this man, Lilly are you aware of this?"

I could see his neck again now, that temptation to which I hadn't succumbed. But if Martin hadn't been there, what would've happened? Would I have bitten this man to feed or to hide my secret? It could be like this every time that danger came my way. Nevertheless, the other evening in the club, nothing had happened to me. Why, this time, had I felt the need to defend myself?

"Your life was in danger, that's why you reacted that way. The instinct of self-preservation, you understand?" He continued.

"You're not angry?"

"No, but this demonstrates that you'll still need us for some while before walking straight out among human beings. We still have things to show you. After all, you're still very young," he smiled.

"I don't want this instinct!" I said sadly.

"You have no choice Lilly, it's within you."

He lifted up my chin and stared me right in the eyes.

"Every being possesses an instinct for survival. You just have to learn to manage it, because for us, it has to remain hidden. We'll survive on the sole condition that we don't feed on humans. Our instinct represents our danger. We're here to show you the path, don't forget this."

On these words, he took me in his arms.

18

"A surprising medical discovery, which is attributed to Professor Moonroe, of the Pasteur of Neuilly private hospital, offers a glimpse of real hope for all the people affected by multiple illnesses. Indeed, one of his patients has been totally cured; as announced in a dispatch on Thursday from AFP. This person, affected by several diseases and a victim of a stroke, has completely recovered.

This miracle is down to the care and medication lavished on the patient by Professor Moonroe, as well as the exemplary lifestyle of the patient herself, over the last six months. This gives an immense hope to other sick patients.

The person who was miraculously cured didn't wish to comment on the subject, and Professor Moonroe remains unreachable at the time of announcing this news."

I went over to Darren, who was sitting in an armchair, a magazine open in his hands. I put my hands around his shoulders and read the article which he was glancing at.

"He came out with it," he announced.

"So I see. It's not good news."

"Its good news that he's alive, but I'd like to know why he's hiding. Hasn't he tried to contact you?"

"No. Do you believe we should be looking for him?"

"I'm going to discuss it with Martin."

His mobile phone rang. He retrieved it from the coffee table.

"Hello? Yes Martin, I've read it. It's annoying indeed."

He stood up and went over to the window. I could see by his grave expression, that Martin didn't look favourably upon the way Moonroe had acted either. He'd remained silent for several weeks before re-surfacing via the press. Nothing augured well. On the day of the incident in his office, we had thought it would give us a bit of time, but he'd never contacted me again and had never given me any news. Now, he was acting slyly from his corner. The wheels had been set in motion without us being able to react.

Even if he was hiding, he was now under the spotlight thanks to this announcement. At least within the medical environment. We hadn't seen anything coming, but we needed to know what he knew or believed he knew, and especially what he was plotting.

Darren hung up, turned to me and hinted at a smile.

"I could really do with a coffee," he exclaimed, contrary to all expectations.

"Why not?" I answered, following him into the kitchen; Hector's kingdom.

Hector wasn't there and I could see Darren rummaging through the cupboards. He did amuse me.

"Difficult to find one's things in one's own kitchen, right?"

"Don't laugh," he said, opening another cupboard.

At this precise moment, Hector made his entrance. I heard Darren's sigh of relief.

"I'll take care of it! Go and sit down," he said in a strict tone of voice.

I took my place with Darren on the high stools arranged around the central island. He remained silent.

Hector put our coffees down in front of us and went out into the garden.

"What did Martin say to you?"

"We have to find this man. Martin is going to consult his medical contacts, he'll use his powers of persuasion to glean some information. You, you're going to call his secretary and ask for an appointment. After that, we'll see."

"Okay, I'll fetch my telephone."

A few minutes later, I was again sitting in front of Darren. I dialled the number.

"It's ringing," I whispered, activating the loudspeaker.

A female voice answered.

"Doctor Schwartz's secretary, how may I help you?"

"Hello, I must've made a mistake about the number... I was trying to contact Professor Moonroe."

"Following his attack, Professor Moonroe left long-term. Do you wish to have an appointment with Doctor Schwartz?"

"I don't know... Does he have the files of Professor Moonroe's patients? I don't want to have to tell my whole story one more time!"

"Yes, naturally. What's your name, please?"

I questioned Darren with a look. He gave me his agreement with a nod.

"Connolly. With two N's and two L's!"

Darren opened his eyes widely; it was true that he didn't know my name. I placed my hand over the telephone.

"What?"

"You're Irish?"

"It's a long story. Wait, she's speaking to me."

I turned aside in order to concentrate.

"Lilly…?" Asked the secretary.

"Yes, that's it."

A glimmer of hope! I could hear her tapping on her keyboard whilst making strange noises with her mouth.

"Oh, this is strange… You were a patient of the professor for a long time, but except for the date of your first meeting, I can find nothing about your pathology. Nothing attached to the file, just a comment which dates back a few days. "Patient cured" has been added to it."

"Who wrote that?"

"The professor himself. He must have done it from his home. Why do you wish to see him again, since you're cured? You are, aren't you?"

"Yes, I am," I said happily, "but I didn't have time to properly thank the professor. Would you have an address or a phone number you could give me, so that I might be able to do so?"

"I don't know whether I'm authorised…"

"Please, he did so much for me! I'm certain that he'd be pleased."

"What you're asking me for, are his private address and phone number" she replied.

"Listen to me: The professor took care of me for years. He cured me, saved my life, you understand? I have to express my gratitude to him. A few words and some flowers will please him. It's not much, compared to a life, but well… Help me, please."

A long silence descended on the other end of the line. I let her consider my arguments.

"Well, all right," she murmured finally. "But tell nobody, I could get fired! Do you have something to write with?"

"Yes, one moment, if I may."

I took the paper and pen which Darren handed to me. He was also smiling.

"I'm back with you."

"He lives at 235, Rue de la Rivière Argentée in Neuilly. I only have his mobile number."

"That's perfect, I'm listening to you."

"06 72 53 53 00. Above all, don't mention this to anybody," she repeated fearfully.

She hung up immediately. I didn't even have time to thank her. I was left speechless, with my eyes open big and round. Darren came over and wrapped his arms around me.

"We have the information which we wanted. The rest doesn't matter, Lilly. What's more, you were convincing," he murmured in my ear.

"It wasn't very difficult, admit it. What are we going to do, now?"

"Tell me first: You're Irish?"

I smiled. I knew that he'd remember that.

"Yes, curious one, my father was Irish. From Galway. Unfortunately for me, my parents remained married only long enough to conceive me. Ephemeral love; how my mother likes it. I bear only his name, I know nothing else about him. There, are you satisfied?"

"For the time being, yes. One day, I'll take you to Ireland, we'll find your father. If you wish to, of course!"

"Maybe… We'll see. Are you ready to answer me, now that you've satisfied your curiosity? What are we going to do with this information? I'm talking about Moonroe's address!"

"I'm going to discuss it with Martin."

I stepped back a little.

"I want to come with you. I don't want him to be hurt."

In my mind I could still hear Marie's words suggesting the death of the professor in case of any trouble.

"Do you understand me?"

"Yes, I understand you," he said, looking downwards. "Don't worry about him. Not yet."

While I was frowning, waiting to see what was coming next, he continued calmly.

"If – and I mean "if" – he's a threat to our community, we'll have to act. If he's reasonable, his life will be spared. Do you also understand?"

"Yes, but promise me that absolutely every effort will be made to avoid this man's death. Promise me, Darren!"

He raised his hand as if taking an oath.

"I promise you," he said seriously. "Now, excuse me, I must call Martin."

On these words, he left the room, leaving me alone. My eyes stared into the distance, I barely saw the magnificent gardens so well maintained by Hector and his wife. I saw the gardener without looking at him, and when I became aware of his presence nearby, I went to join him, to question him a little. Provided that Hector would be receptive, because he wasn't very communicative. Since my arrival in the chateau, he'd improved a little, becoming used to my presence, but after the ball and my more than obvious closeness with

Darren, he'd kept his distance a little. He respected me as if I were Darren's wife, which was far from being the case. Furthermore, he had no reason to dedicate the same loyalty to me as he did to Darren.

Contrary to all expectations, Darren and I were irresistibly attracted to one another. It went back to our very first meeting, almost to when we first set eyes on each other. I think that without this attraction, he wouldn't have transformed me. He'd done it on my demand, an extremely rare request. I can remember very well the problem it created on Pierre's birthday, and during the council which Marie unexpectedly demanded on the evening of my introduction to the rest of the family. My entry into the family hadn't been without turmoil.

But soon, I'd return to live in my own home, far away from him. We'd see whether, at this time, separated from each other, our feelings would remain the same. I didn't just like him because he was my creator, but for what he was; a whole, generous being: Also, which did nothing to spoil it, with a rare beauty. For the time being, we'd let things be. We had plenty of time. What we were living through made me happy, we had the whole of eternity to either love or hate each other.

I approached Hector. He was wrapping the shrubs with some plastic so that they could withstand the frost and emerge from it big and strong. He was so conscientious…! I watched him with admiration.

"Hector, we have a problem with Professor Moonroe."

I didn't know if he knew about our business, or even if he was interested in it. He appeared distant from it all!

"I know, Miss Lilly. Human beings remain unpredictable. But don't worry, Darren's going to take care of it."

I looked at him in astonishment: This was the first time I'd heard Hector refer to Darren by his first name. He was in the habit of saying Sir.

"I know, and that's what frightens me: I don't want that we hurt this man."

"He won't hurt him, rest assured," he asserted, pushing his wheelbarrow full of things towards the next shrub.

"How can you be so sure about that?"

"I just know, that's all."

"I won't be content with that, as you well know!"

I positioned myself to face him. He had no way out, he sighed noisily. Apparently, to go into the matter any deeper was disturbing him. I therefore insisted.

"What are you trying to say?"

"That Sir is a good person. He wouldn't harm a human, he'd try to make him see sense."

"And if he doesn't succeed?"

Hector remained silent, he pretended to concentrate on his shrub. I didn't give in either. He raised his head towards me following a few minutes of an oppressive silence.

"I doubt that, Miss."

"But if not! What would happen then?"

"Why always imagine failure?"

He frowned. I sensed that he was hiding something.

"I'm just envisaging all the possibilities. So, if he fails, such that the professor continues his research and discovers us, what'll happen? How can we stop him at this point?"

He held his arms suspended in mid-air, interrupted in his movements. Then, he gave me a look as cold as ice.

"Ask Darren. I have work to do, I'm sorry. See him about it."

He put his tools down straight away, removed his gloves which he threw on the wheelbarrow, and left in the direction of Amélie's greenhouse. He left me with no answers, just a multitude of further questions.

I was going back to the chateau, when I saw Darren sitting in his car. I ran up to meet him and positioned myself in front of the bonnet. My expression said enough. He looked at me for a few seconds through the windscreen, then got out and came over to me. When he got close to me, he held my face between his hands and said calmly:

"Let's get this straight, Lilly. I made you a promise, you have to trust me."

"Let me come along with you, please. You're going to see Martin, right?"

"Yes, then I'm coming back and we'll discuss it together."

"No, I want to come, this is my concern. All of this occurred because of me, I won't be pushed aside."

"Lilly…" He sighed. "Let us devise a plan between us. I'll be returning within two hours at the latest. Find yourself something to do, calm down, and then we'll talk to each other."

I stared him right in the eyes, my whole being wanted to accompany him, to say no to him, but I sensed that there was no point in insisting. I caught myself saying to him with a sigh:

"All right, Darren…"

He planted a kiss on my lips and sat back behind the steering wheel. My gaze remained glued to his car until it disappeared. I regained my senses at this moment. Darren had manipulated my will to make me accept this in spite of myself. I felt anger welling up inside me, but an observation immediately dawned on me: Darren's dissuasive power was immense, but it lost its effect when he went away.

It made me curious and almost led me to forget me why he'd used this gift on me. So I went up to my bedroom and settled myself down on the bed. I opened the book that would teach me more about this particular gift, which perhaps I too had inherited.

I didn't notice time passing. The daylight was vanishing, the two hours had now mostly gone. I delicately put the precious tome on the bed and went over to check out the horizon. From my window, I could see the road beyond the limits of the property. The round lights of Darren's headlights finally appeared. I followed the bright beams of light right up to the courtyard.

A few moments later, he knocked on my door. I invited him to come in, without a smile. He came over to me.

"Excuse me, I had no choice. I had to go there alone," he said gently.

"We always have a choice. However, I don't hold it against you, because your behaviour allowed me to find out more about your gift; I wondered if I too possessed it. According to the book, it's highly likely that I do."

He seemed amazed.

"You're not angry? Really?"

"No, I'm not. I did what you told me: I waited. And for much longer than two hours, besides."

I had to remark upon his delay.

"I occupied myself by reading, I put my anger aside. Now, it's up to you to keep to your commitment: What happened with Martin?"

He turned to face the park and stared off into the distance. Then, in a calm tone, he began to describe his talk with Martin.

"As you're able to grasp, we have to meet Moonroe to verify what he does or doesn't know; whether he's still under the impression that he's made an important medical discovery, or whether he suspects that we exist. For the moment, we favour the first hypothesis. Considering the AFP news, nothing leads us to suppose anything else. But we're only extrapolating from these fragments of information. As he knows Martin, I'm going to meet him myself by making him think that I'm a journalist. We arranged a meeting tomorrow morning at eleven o'clock in the Café de la Marquise, in Neuilly. So, I can sound him out..."

"To sound him out...? What do you mean?"

"To read his mind, Lilly," he said, smiling. "You know...What I do all the time with you, and which you hate."

"Ah! That... Indeed, I do hate it! In doing that, you see into my private thoughts," I answered, pretending to be outraged.

He was still smiling. He pulled me over to him. His heat invaded me. I continued:

"Besides, you; you close your mind most of the time, which I find to be unfair."

He placed a hand on my head and gently shook it, laughing.

"Yes, but one day, you'll have access there. Don't be in such a hurry to hear it all. I can be intrusive, you know!"

"I doubt it. Really, I doubt it."

I stood on tiptoe to place a gentle kiss on his cheek.

"I presume that I won't be able to accompany you tomorrow either, seeing that he knows me?"

"No. We have to be sure to stay credible. On the other hand..."

"On the other hand...?"

"You could position yourself nearby and listen to the conversation?"

"Would you would permit me to?"

"If I've proposed it to you, then yes of course. But on one condition."

I knew very well that there would be a "but"!

"You don't move! You don't intervene, whatever he says or whatever takes place. You must promise me, Lilly."

He fixed me, waiting for my answer. I raised my right hand, which I then placed on his chest.

"I promise you."

"Perfect. The case is closed for the moment. I'm going to leave you presently. You should rest: A long and tiring day awaits us tomorrow. And next, I have to inquire a bit more into this man: I'm supposed to be a medical journalist. However, if I know nothing of his speciality, I'm quickly going to be unmasked."

"All right. Good night, Darren."

I accompanied him as far as the door. When he was acting like this, it was pointless to insist. He'd decided to leave, and I should let him do it. Smiling, he squeezed my hand and disappeared down to the end of the corridor. He was heading towards the library.

19

Ten o'clock on the dot. We were driving towards Neuilly. A tape recorder over his shoulder and his press card around his neck, Darren was every bit the perfect journalist. He was dressed in a navy blue shirt, a black jacket and, the least unexpected detail; a pair of glasses. His rather successful disguise amused me.

I wore a hat to hide my long brown hair, a big pair of black glasses as well as a long coat, black also. Moonroe mustn't recognise me, or even notice me; it would put Darren's operation in danger. And since I couldn't be too far from them in order to hear them, and possibly intervene…

The journey went well. Darren parked not far from where the appointment was to be, it was ten forty-five am. As agreed, I got out first and went quietly over to the corner of the street, from where I could see the cafe. I'd have to wait for them to settle into their places before I'd be able to find an adequate place for myself. Darren would keep Moonroe occupied enough so that he wouldn't notice my entry.

I didn't have to wait for a long time, because the professor was punctual on this day, compared with the appointments in his medical practice. He opened the door at eleven o'clock sharp and joined Darren at the end table, where he'd sat down just a few minutes ago. They'd arranged it the day before over the telephone. In any case, he was recognisable with his tape recorder.

Darren stood up and shook hands with him. This was the signal for me to come into the cafe. While I was crossing the street, I saw them sit back down again. Moonroe turned his back to the door.

My choice came down to a table on the other side of the bar, in a small recess. I took out a magazine which I pretended to look through, and ordered a white coffee and a glass of water. Now that I was settled, I could concentrate on what was being said a few metres away from me. I could see them by tilting myself backwards a little on my chair and by looking towards the back of the bar.

Darren introduced himself and tried to win the professor's confidence. Moonroe didn't seem to be wary. Then, Darren explained to him how the interview was going to take place. At this precise moment, he started up the tape recorder, stating that he could switch off it at any time if Moonroe wished. What's more, He put his finger on the red stop button.

"I have nothing to hide," said Moonroe, removing Darren's finger.

At this point, I wondered if he'd noticed the coldness of Darren's skin, just like I'd felt it the first time my skin had been in contact with his.

"Very good. In that case, let's begin," he answered very professionally. "I read on a dispatch from AFP that you think you've made an incredible discovery with a case of multiple diseases that have been completely cured. It concerned one of your long-term patients. Can you tell me why you consider yourself responsible for this cure and what kind of treatment you gave her?"

Darren smiled to him and nodded his head to encourage him to speak. However, Moonroe didn't answer. He seemed to be searching for words, stroking his hand on his chin. He drank a mouthful of the coffee which the waiter had just brought.

"Well," he finally began. "This patient, who I've looked after for years, following a stroke which she had very young, came to see me a few weeks ago for a bi-annual check-up."

Darren nodded his head, to encourage him to continue.

"She was well. To each one of my questions, her answer was the same: Everything was good."

"In what way was this surprising?"

"To get better, why not? But to appear cured, when a few months earlier, she was ever so ill! Next, the clinical examination went perfectly, even though she'd tried at times to persuade me to the contrary. I wasn't fooled, you know!" He said, winking.

"I'm certain of it, professor. Why did she act this way in your opinion?"

"Good question!" Moonroe exclaimed noisily.

I looked at him, he began to fidget. This would be interesting. They stayed silent for a moment, then he started again:

"When I asked her if she was taking her medicine, she maintained that she was."

He bent over the table and whispered:

"I found no trace of it, anywhere in her blood test. Her treatment is too strong for her body to assimilate everything. She's taken it for such a long time! It's impossible for there not to have been even the slightest trace."

He sat back down on his chair and added, as if it was obvious:

"Her blood was clean, pure!"

"Why do you claim this success when, at the end of the day, she's neither taken her medicine nor anything else, besides? How do you explain her cure?"

"We aren't cured by magic, Sir!"

He looked all around, because he'd just realised to what extent he'd raised his voice. I hid behind my magazine. He finished his coffee and started again:

"On the day of my attack, I was taking a new blood sample myself, to ensure that nothing or nobody could intervene on this sample. The first test had been changed, or something like that, I'm sure. That was the reason why I wanted to see her again."

Moonroe seemed more and more crazy. Darren would have to, more than ever, remain prudent in the way he'd ask his questions.

"What did you find, this time, in the results?"

"Still no trace of her medicine, but an enzyme which was completely unknown to me. Was it this enzyme which destroyed the medicine? Was this what had cured her? I admit to not knowing this for the time being. I'm continuing in my research."

"Why do you hide yourself, professor? To divulge the evolution of your research and your discoveries would allow you to obtain grants. Maybe another researcher is about to discover something on the subject?"

"No, no, no. I don't need help from anybody. I want to clarify this mystery myself. I'm certain that I'm about to make an important discovery, essential in the type of research which I've undertaken for years. It's out of the question to share this glory with anyone."

This avarice and sheer human greed was the pinnacle of his stupidity! Nothing astonished me more. But above all, this man was becoming crazy and his madness could turn out to be dangerous for our community, or simply for me, because, in a few days' time, I'd be confronted alone by this very individual.

"Would you want to grant me exclusivity?" Darren then asked.

He answered in a haughty tone, as if the glory was already waiting at his door:

"I can't promise you that..."

"Tell me, Professor Moonroe, what kind of attack did you have?"

"A light stroke, but I suffer no after-effects, as you can see Sir."

Darren smiled: What Moonroe took to be a light stroke was in fact a passive neutralisation done by Martin, on the day of the appointment. It was our only solution, because I had been transforming myself and Moonroe couldn't have been allowed to witness it.

"Indeed, professor, no visible after-effects. Was it predictable?"

"Not really. I still don't understand why this happened to me. You know, the human body sometimes brings us surprises," he concluded.

Darren switched off his tape recorder and decreed that it would suffice for this time. Moonroe gave him his business card with his email address, so that Darren could send him the so-called article. They shook hands and left.

When I was certain that he wouldn't return, I joined Darren at his table.

"This man is crazy!" I told him as discreetly as possible.

"I'm afraid so, yes. Martin ought to have him committed. He doesn't suspect what he's really discovered, but he's still dangerous. There are quite a lot of vampires in the medical world and I'm very much afraid that one day, Moonroe will cause us more problems than he does now. Thanks to his attack, I think that Martin can find a good reason for committing him or for obliging him to take a forced rest, far away from everything."

"You're right, it's a way of neutralising him without killing him. Thank you, Darren," I said sincerely.

"You see, I had promised you that I wouldn't hurt him."

He stood up and offered me his hand.

"Let's go home, this madman has exhausted me. His head's full of words which mean nothing. In any case, not in the sense which he thinks they mean," he exclaimed, bursting out laughing.

Epilogue

Three days later, Darren announced that Martin had committed Moonroe into a rest home in Switzerland. In the end, it'd been simpler than anticipated, thanks partially to the professor's wife, who was very worried about her husband's mental health. This permitted me to return to my life in a more serene way.

I was in the process of gathering my things together. Everything came back to me all at once: The last few weeks of my new life; so rich, and then Darren. We'd avoided the subject. Our relationship had changed so much! It had, that too, been enriched so much by everything. An unwavering friendship, a flourishing love, a strong link which united us forever. Today, this predicted separation, known about since the first moment, and which we were dreading so much, had arrived. I was lost in my thoughts when he knocked. I raised my head sadly.

"Yes…?"

"It's me! He announced through the chink of the door. Am I disturbing you?"

"Of course not."

He made his way into the room and quickly looked at my things. I sensed his waft of sadness.

"Here we are," he said simply.

"I'm afraid so, yes. You know, when I leave a place, I always take a souvenir with me. My bathroom is full of them," I said, trying to smile.

He came over to me and asked me in all seriousness:

"What would you like to take away from my bathroom, Lilly?"

"I don't know… I'd very much like to say the bathtub, but that might be complicated. Let me think for a few moments…"

Without leaving me any time to think, he went into the bathroom and returned, with his hands behind his back.

"Close your eyes and hold out your hands," he told me.

I did so, and felt a heavy rounded object. My hands felt all over it and I recognised the jar of bath salts. I smiled at the memory which it brought back into my head: My immersion, the challenge that I'd given myself to hold on for as long as possible… I'd already almost forgotten this great moment of discovery, on my first day as a vampire.

Darren interrupted my flashback by planting a kiss on my lips. I reopened my eyes and smiled to him. I was going to miss him.

"Thank you Darren, this object is going to outclass all my other souvenirs. I'm going to find it a place of significance, like the place which you've taken in my life and in my heart. A place which outshines all the rest. It pleases me very much."

"I know."

"You…?"

He places a finger on my mouth and embraced me. I closed my eyes and immersed myself in him one last time. We didn't know when we'd see each other again. We hadn't spoken about anything. The subject had remained taboo, deep in our hearts.

"Lilly," he mumbled, "never, really never, had I imagined I'd meet a person like you, so human, so stubborn, so tenacious, and yet so fragile…"

He cleared his throat; he was a little embarrassed.

"You don't have to, Darren…"

"It's true, little Lilly, nothing obliges me to tell you how much you mean to me. But I need to, you understand? What you brought, what you bring to my eternal life, is much more than you might think. You're not simply the person who wanted to become like us, you became entirely one of us. Now, you're here, you're a part of my life and I admit that I'm going to miss you. I wanted you to know that I'll never be far away, that if you need me, all you have to do is call. On that subject…"

He began searching in his pocket and brought out a telephone.

"Here's a telephone which has a location system. That way, I can locate you at any moment, should it be necessary. I've saved the numbers for Vic, the club, the chateau and myself."

I took the little jewel of technology which he handed me. The word "Smartphone" took on all its meaning when I briefly examined the device. The location option was perhaps only the simplest of its applications!

"Thank you, Darren. You mean so very much to me too. Much more than my words could describe right now."

I snuggled up to him. Tears welled up inside me, but I didn't want him to see me crying. I was sad, very sad. He hugged me even more tightly, such that I almost suffocated.

"Be careful, Lilly, promise me."

"Don't worry."

"Yes, justifiably, I do worry! You haven't much experience... I didn't have time to show you, to..."

I interrupted him.

"I've seen what the humans are capable of. I'll be careful, Darren. You can, very much so too, call me to hear my news or simply to talk to me. Darren..."

I couldn't finish my sentence, his lips were glued to mine, closing a conversation which was going round in circles. It would've been simpler just to say that we love each other, but that was neither his style nor mine. Besides, these three words did no justice to how we felt.

At dawn, my eyes misty with emotion, I took one last look at the big house.

I saw Darren behind the library window. I stayed there, frozen, just looking at him.

"Don't forget me, Darren, I..."

Without waiting for an answer from him, I sat myself in my car and gently pressed down on the accelerator. Passing through the gates of the chateau, as usual, I put my foot down all the way to the floor. At that moment, his voice resounded in my head:

"I can't, and I especially don't want to, my Lilly!"

It was with a smile on my lips, and in my heart, that I headed onto the motorway. My new life began right now.